Marguerite Tollemache

Spanish Mystics

Marguerite Tollemache

Spanish Mystics

ISBN/EAN: 9783337369415

Printed in Europe, USA, Canada, Australia, Japan

Cover: Foto ©Andreas Hilbeck / pixelio.de

More available books at **www.hansebooks.com**

SPANISH MYSTICS

A SEQUEL TO 'MANY VOICES'

BY THE SAME WRITER

'If any man hear My voice, and open the door,
I will come in to him'

Rev. iii. 20

LONDON

KEGAN PAUL, TRENCH, & CO., 1 PATERNOSTER SQUARE

1886

'Blessed are the ears which vibrate to the pulses of the Divine Whisper'—THOMAS À KEMPIS

'These have sweet life in different degrees,
By feeling more or less the Eternal Breath'

DANTE, *Paradise* (Canto IV.)

THE following extracts have been selected from the works of Spanish Mystics of the sixteenth and seventeenth centuries, whose writings are perhaps less known to the English reader than the works of our own religious writers of the same period.

'Très-pauvre de substance, je ne me croyais propre
qu'aux travaux de compilation.'

INTRODUCTION.

MYSTICISM has been termed 'the natural produce of the soil of Spain.'[1] It breathes not only in her theology, but in her literature and in her fine arts.

Sharp contrasts of climate, tastes, and habits are to be found in the different provinces of the Iberian Peninsula, but to the student of Spanish history one prevailing element pervades the whole and seems to unite the opposing forces.[2] It is this religious sentiment which is everywhere predominant, and which has ever formed an integral part of the national character.

In the early annals of Spain the nation was not exempt from the taint of Arianism ; but when, in the sixth century, under her Gothic king, Recared, she renounced its errors and accepted the orthodox faith preached by Leander and Isidore, every power was thenceforth devoted to the maintenance of that Catholic faith with which her greatness became indissolubly united. The wars which she waged were in defence of orthodoxy. To defend her

[1] See *History of Spanish Literature* (Ticknor).
[2] See *Les Mystiques espagnols* (Paul Rousselot).

religion was to defend herself. The faith which she upheld enabled her to reconquer her soil from the infidel, and under the sacred banner of the Cross she drove forth both the Moor and the Jew. It followed almost of necessity that intolerance became a Christian virtue in the eyes of the Spaniard. In vain had Isidore, the saintly Archbishop of Seville, denounced the use of force as contrary to the spirit of Christianity; the demon of persecution was let loose in the land, and stalked abroad seeking whom to devour.

The Jews were the first victims to this religious zeal; but in the eighth century the Gothic rule came to an end. The Arabs entered Spain from the south; Roderic, the last of the Gothic kings, vanquished at the battle of Guadalete, fled from the scene of his disaster to perish ignobly in the waters of the Guadalquivir.[1]

The persecuted Jews took part with the Moslems. Through their help Granada, Cordova, and Toledo (the royal city) fell into the hands of the invaders, and those Christians who would not submit to the yoke of the Moslem took refuge in the mountains and fastnesses of the northern provinces.[2] But, though forced to retreat before the intruding Moors, these Christian Spaniards never submitted to their infidel foes. Pent up in the mountains of the Pyrenees, they looked back with longing gaze on the vineyards and olive gardens of which they had been despoiled. Led on by their priests, and with the name of St. Iago, the patron saint of Spain, as their war-cry, they

[1] See *Decline and Fall* (Gibbon).
[2] Some even made their way to Ireland, and Galway still bears testimony to this fact. See *Ferdinand and Isabella* (Prescott).

made constant incursions into the conquered provinces, so that in the succeeding century they had won back a considerable portion of Castile. Toledo was recovered in 1085, and the Moors were thrust back into the southern provinces. Jews and Moslems were now alike odious to the Spaniard, and the renowned Cid, the national hero of the eleventh century, is still enshrined in the hearts of his countrymen not only as the defender of the faith, but as the despoiler of the Jew. Granada—the last stronghold of the Moors—was captured in 1492 ; but with this landmark in Spanish history is associated the spread of that terrible instrument of intolerance, the Spanish Inquisition. It had already existed for two centuries in Aragon and Catalonia ; in 1478 it had been admitted into Castile ;[1] it was now extended by Sixtus IV. to the fair lands of the South. Granada, Valencia, and all the Moorish provinces were placed under its jurisdiction at the request of Isabella—' as a pious gift to her people '—and every mosque was destroyed or converted into a Christian church.

From early ages the Church had been accepted in Spain as the governing power of the State. Superior in learning and in the art of government, she held both kings and nobles under her sway. Submission to her dictates was a law engraven on the hearts of all devout Spaniards, and the establishment of the Inquisition had increased her power tenfold. The discovery of the new world by Columbus, which quickly followed the conquest of Granada, gave untold wealth to Spain, but the influx of gold deteriorated the national character. Rapacity and inhumanity marked

---

[1] It was instituted by Gregory IX. in 1232. See *British and Foreign Review*, No. 15, 1839.

the Spanish conquests, and left an indelible stain on the nation.

After the death of Cardinal Mendoza in 1494, Ximenes, the ascetic Franciscan monk, became Primate and Prime Minister of Spain, and on the demise of Ferdinand the Catholic, he was named Regent of Castile and Aragon during the short minority of Ferdinand's grandson, the future Emperor Charles V.

Rank vices and abuses had sprung up in the Church, and Ximenes, whilst with the one hand he fought the Barbary Moors, with the other strove to check the growing immorality of the monastic orders. He instituted rigorous reforms among the Franciscans, of which order he was Provincial, and expelled from the monasteries the refractory monks who refused to turn from their evil ways.[1] The ignorance of the clergy was another evil with which Ximenes had to cope, and to him Spain owes the first impulse given in this century to sacred learning. He revived the study of Greek and Hebrew, long neglected in her schools, and to his munificence his countrymen are indebted for the University of Alcala, built at his expense and richly endowed with valuable manuscripts.

He especially encouraged Biblical study, and from Alcala issued forth in 1514 the famous Polyglot Bible, known as the Complutensium.[2] The invention of printing in the preceding century had opened the flood-gates of know-ledge : hidden treasures were now revealed to the world, and the intellectual movement which followed spread with

---

[1] See *Cloister Life of Charles V.* (Stirling).

[2] The Complutensium was printed in 1514, but the publication was delayed till 1522. It was designed after the Hexapla of Origen.

rapid strides throughout Europe. But whilst in other lands mental vigour was fast developing, in Spain its progress was stayed by the strong arm of the Inquisition. Lutheran tracts had made their way into the Peninsula, and the minds of men were astir. But the whole power of the State and of the Holy Office was at once exerted to crush the seeds of 'heresy' before they could take root in Spanish soil.

Men of learning were especially regarded with jealousy and suspicion. Intellectual freedom was trampled under foot. Stringent orders were given to search out all heretical books ; no works were suffered to be published or imported without the sanction of the Holy Office ; and the penalty of death was decreed against those who should disseminate 'the new doctrines.'

'Cut out this root of evil,' had been the counsel of Charles V. a few months before his death at Yuste in 1558, and the fires and dungeons of the Inquisition did the work effectually.[1] Lutheranism was extinguished in Catholic Spain, but with it had perished some of the best and wisest of the land, and all freedom of thought. Spanish literature thus received its death-blow, whilst that of other nations was acquiring fresh vitality. In the words of a great French writer, 'Not genius, but liberty, was wanting in Spain.'[2]

The need of reform in the Church had long been felt in the Peninsula. From many a lowly cell prayers had been breathed forth for a spiritual and moral renovation. Laymen and ecclesiastics had alike rebuked with voice and

---

[1] See *Cloister Life of Charles V.* (Stirling).
[2] M. R. Saint-Hilaire.

pen the immorality which prevailed in the various orders of
the Church.[1] Here and there men had arisen and established partial reforms in the orders to which they belonged,
but the evil was not cast out. The demoralised state of
the Spanish clergy, both regular and secular, was a national
disgrace. The education of the young was committed to
the monastic orders, but the cloister had lost its purity.
The evil contracted within the walls of the convent spread
but too often to the family, and parents sighed over the
pernicious influence to which their children were exposed,
but none devised a remedy.[2]

Then arose Teresa of Avila—high-souled, impassioned,
heroic—who believed that Divine love in the heart could
alone stem the tide of sin, and by her—one of the leading
spirits of her country in the sixteenth century—was accomplished a revival of religion and virtue in the Spanish
Church. Her appearance marked a new spiritual epoch.
Like Deborah of old, she raised a cry which awoke the
nation from its death-like slumber. The reform of the
Catholic Church through the reform of the cloister was the
great end ever before her, and the special work which
Teresa undertook was the reform of the Carmelite Order, to
which she herself belonged. The fervour of her piety and
the devotion of her life soon kindled a flame which spread
from heart to heart. She collected together the forces
which were to fight the battle of the Lord—men who had
the witness of the Spirit within themselves, and whose
weapons were not carnal, but mighty through God to the

[1] See *Cloister Life of Charles V.*
[2] See *Œuvres très-complètes de Ste. Thérèse*, &c. (Abbé Migne).

pulling down of strongholds. In the power of a life filled and possessed by the Spirit of God her missionaries went forth to bring light to lands where there was only darkness, and to proclaim the fulness of the blessing of the Gospel of Christ to souls degraded and enslaved by sin. But this was not all. Within the walls of the cloister, where a moral plague had lately infected the whole atmosphere, a mighty change was wrought. Purity of conventual life was restored, and in those sanctuaries where profane talk and secular amusements had filled up the greater portion of the daily life, the voice of prayer now ascended continually for the spiritual and moral reform of the Church and the world.

This was the mission accomplished by Teresa. In her, Spanish Mysticism found its most ardent exponent. She arrested the spreading evil of formalism in religion by teaching her followers to seek God *within*, in that hidden sanctuary where the soul finds its Divine Lord and enters into spiritual contact and union with Him.

In an age when words were weighed and sifted, and all liberty of speech was repressed, this secret life—called Mysticism—opened to men a safe and silent retreat. In that inner chamber of the soul, where ' they might turn the key, and none could enter,' they were still free. They were able—' unheard by all but angel ears '—to pour forth their pent-up thoughts and feelings to that Divine Lord whose living personal Presence was to them a reality ; and as earth receded they were given ecstatic moments, when heaven opened to their gaze and they were admitted to the Beatific Vision.

As our minds dwell on these enraptured saints and

Mystics, we cannot but feel that there are heights and depths in the spiritual life which confound the wisdom of the wise and set at nought the understanding of the prudent. They saw what many have desired to see and have not seen, and heard what many have desired to hear and have not heard; and we, seeing as yet but through a glass darkly, must be content to wait and watch in meekness and patience till for us also 'the day break and the shadows flee away.'

Ӎ

March 1886.

CONTENTS.

———•◦•———

SPANISH MYSTICS

SAN PEDRO DE ALCANTARA.

B. 1499.   D. 1562.

' LET him who desires to advance on the road to virtue not start without the spur of devotion ; for otherwise he will altogether fail to make his stumbling, ill-conditioned beast hold up.'

'It is as necessary to regulate the heart before prayer and meditation as to tune the guitar before playing it.'

'In prayer the soul renews its youth and regains its freshness.'

'Beware of spending so much time in devotional *reading* as thereby to hinder devout *meditation*, this last being a more fruitful exercise, inasmuch as those things on which we attentively reflect sink deeper and produce greater results.'

'In meditation let the person rouse himself from things temporal, and let him *collect himself within himself*—that is to say, within the very centre of his soul, where lies impressed the image of God. Here let him hearken to the voice of God as though speaking to him from on high, yet present in his soul, and as though there were no other in the world save God and himself.'

B

'In meditation we must act like a wise gardener who, when he watereth a plot of ground, waiteth a while after the first sprinkling of water until it be soaked in, and then sprinkleth again, so that the earth may be thoroughly wet and thus become more fruitful.'

'We must use special caution in speaking to others of those hidden consolations with which Almighty God hath been pleased to refresh our souls.   Even as that mellifluous doctor—St. Bernard—was wont to advise everyone to have these words in large letters written in his room, "MY SECRET TO MYSELF."'

Pedro de Alcantara was so named from his birthplace, the ancient town of Alcantara, in the province of Estremadura.   Once a frontier stronghold of the great military order of Alcantara, it is now desolate and deserted.   Ruined walls and towers and what was once a stately convent still crown the craggy height overlooking the Tagus, but with the old Benedictine knights its glory has departed.

The father of Pedro was governor of Murcia in the reign of Ferdinand and Isabella the Catholic, and both he and his wife being devout persons, they trained up their son from early years in the fear of God.   Pedro studied for some time at Salamanca, but at fourteen he returned to his home, and the divine germ implanted in his soul in child-hood sprang up into vigorous life.   The boy seemed to be filled with the love of God, and from that time forth he renounced the distinction which the world held forth to him and applied his whole mind to the attainment of heavenly wisdom.   He longed for retirement and total seclusion, so that

> . . . separate from the world, his breast
> Might duly take and strongly keep
> The print of Heaven.[1]

---

[1] *Christian Year* (13th Sunday after Trinity).

Accordingly, at the early age of sixteen he entered the lonely Franciscan convent of Manjárez, placed amidst the rugged peaks which rise between Castile and Portugal. There he practised the severest austerities. He restricted his sleep to two hours ; he passed whole days without food. Like the hermits of the Thebaid, he sought to bring his body into complete subjection to the spirit. To lead a life of ceaseless communion with the Unseen, to be for ever consciously enfolded within the Divine Presence—this was his one desire. And in that rocky solitude he waited and watched ; he prayed and fasted till the poor earthly frame of the young devotee grew weak and emaciated, whilst the inner man became luminous with the light of God's countenance.[1]

When he made his profession, he received from his superior the order to go forth and preach. Anointed with spiritual unction, and inspired by Divine love, the young preacher's sermons powerfully affected his hearers, and through his fervour and eloquence many were led to forsake an evil course and live a godly life. At the age of twenty-three he was removed from the convent of Manjárez, and was made superior of his order at Badajoz. It was in the convent of Bellaviz, near Badajoz, after passing long hours in contemplation, that he first received those spiritual manifestations, those revelations of the Lord, which have given him a place among Spanish Mystics. His intense love of seclusion made him request leave to retire to a distant convent at Lapa, near Soriana, where he wrote his book on Prayer, named 'The Golden Book.'

He was deeply versed in Holy Scripture, searching its pages diligently and with extreme reverence. His rule was

---

[1] Pedro is said by his contemporaries to have been so withered and feeble in appearance that he could scarcely drag himself along.

to spend three hours of each day in prayer and meditation, and he was often found rapt in ecstasy, holding blessed communion with his Lord.

The solicitations of John III. of Portugal induced him for a while to leave his retreat and become the king's spiritual director, but he escaped as soon as possible from a post of honour coveted by so many but distasteful to himself, and returned to Spain, where he was appointed Provincial of his order in Estremadura. He saw with sorrow that all religious enthusiasm had died out among his brethren; that cold formalism had taken its place, lying like a dead weight on the souls of men; that they had forsaken the rules of their founder, and had fallen into habits of ease and luxury opposed to the primitive discipline. In 1555 Pedro resolved to commence the work of reform. He drew up a plan which should restore the strict Franciscan rule, and having obtained the sanction of Pope Paul IV. and the consent of his order, he was able to carry out his great scheme, and found the new order of Franciscan friars, called Bare-footed, who should follow closely in the footprints of St. Francis, espousing poverty, and leading lives of the severest self-denial.

When the Emperor Charles V. was established at Yuste, he desired to make Pedro de Alcantara his confessor; but the holy man begged to be left undisturbed in the devotional life which he had adopted. The reform which he instituted among the Franciscans suggested to Teresa of Avila the course which she afterwards adopted with the Carmelites. By her he was ever entitled 'that blessed friar.' She sought his counsel and guidance in her spiritual difficulties, and derived more comfort from him than from any other of her directors. It was to Teresa that Pedro de Alcantara wrote, 'I hold them to be poor in spirit who are broken in will.'

He also told her that one of the greatest trials was the contradiction of good people, and though she had borne much, yet more trouble was in reserve for her.'

In the record of her own life, St. Teresa recounts some of the visions and ecstasies of this holy man, and his supernatural appearance to her when he was at the point of death.[1]

Pedro died in the convent of Mount Areno. It is said that the hour of his death was revealed to him, so that he was able to announce it to those around him.

He received the Holy Sacraments of the Church, and breathed his last devoutly kneeling, and repeating with holy joy the words of the Psalmist :

'I was glad when they said unto me, we will go into the house of the Lord.'[2]

He was canonised by Clement IX. 1669.

JUAN DE AVILA.

B. 1500. D. 1569.

'Love touches the heart far more than benefits, because to do good to others is only giving something of what we possess, whereas in loving we give *ourselves.*'

'Live not in such blindness as to measure the large

---

[1] Pedro de Alcantara is said not only to have appeared, but to have addressed these words to her : 'O felix pœnitentia, quæ tantam mihi promeruit gloriam.'

[2] Teresa, in her *Life*, declares that ' she received even more help and consolation from his ministrations after his entrance into the Heavenly City than when he was on earth.'

hand of God by the niggard rule of your own poor narrow heart.'

'Lament your own misery in the sight of His mercy.'

'It is wholly impossible for a man to be gathering figs from the hand of God whilst he is sowing thorns with his neighbour.'

'Serve not God with a soured heart and drooping wings.'

'To be mightily enraged for every little offence which may be offered us is, as it were, to be giving stabs to our own souls.'

'What marriage is so unhappy as for a man to be wedded to his own will?'

'The enemy that men are to overcome, the city which they are to subdue, is their own self-will. Let them place *that* before them, and AGAINST THAT let them level all their shot. Let them say to it, "Thou art the enemy of God, since thou desirest that which is contrary to Him, and therefore thou art my enemy, for I belong wholly to God."'

'The man who is careful to recollect himself and who puts his confidence in God is ofttimes more recollected in streets and public places than he who remains shut up in his cell.'

'Woe to that soul which presumes to think that he can approach God in any other way than as a sinner asking mercy. *Know* you yourself to be wicked, and God will wrap you up warm in the mantle of His goodness.'

'Know that the man who of all others is most recommended to thy care is *thyself.* For it will profit thee but little, though thou shouldest draw all the world out of the mud, if the while thou thyself remainest therein.'[1]

'If thou desirest to build a house in thy soul for so mighty a Lord, know thou that not the high, but the humble heart is His habitation. Therefore let thy first care be to dig deep down into the earth of thy littleness till, having freed thyself from all self-esteem, thou comest at last to the firm Rock—to God Himself—upon which Rock, and

---

[1] This was written by Juan de Avila to Juan de Dios of Granada, the founder of the order of the 'Caridad,' who had been converted by the preaching of Avila. Juan de Dios was born in Portugal in 1490. His parents were very poor, but they were pious, and brought up their child religiously. When old enough he was sent into the fields to tend the sheep, and would often kneel down and pray as he watched the flock. He grew up and left his home to enlist as a soldier in the army of the Emperor Charles V., and his early thought of God was lost in the strife of the world. Years rolled on, and it was not till he was forty that his conscience awoke from its long torpor. Stung with remorse he resolved to return to his forsaken home in Portugal, and devote the remainder of his days to his parents, and to the service of the poor. He found that his father and mother were dead, and had mourned his loss to the last ; therefore he again wandered forth, and thought to make amends for the past by setting sail for Africa to succour those in slavery. After three years he returned to Spain and settled at Granada. On a certain day, having attended the service of the church, he heard a sermon preached by Juan de Avila, which so profoundly touched him that he burst into tears and cried aloud for mercy as a lost sinner. He was looked upon as mad, and taken to an asylum, from which he was only released through the interference of the great preacher, who perceived that he was not mad, but that his heart had been touched and aroused by the Spirit of God. Avila led him, broken and contrite in spirit, to the Saviour, and peace flowed into Juan's soul. He now hired a small house, and made it a refuge for the sick and destitute. All day long he waited on them, and at night he would go forth and fetch home others, sometimes carrying them on his back. He died in 1550, through plunging into the river Xenil to save a drowning child. The numberless Homes and Refuges which are now to be seen throughout Christendom date from this house of charity founded by Juan de Dios. In the Hospital of the 'Caridad' in Seville there is a picture by Murillo of Juan de Dios bearing home on his back, in a stormy night, a dying beggar.

not upon thine own shifting sand, thou art to build thy house.'

'Know that He who drew thee out of darkness into His marvellous light, and of an enemy made thee a friend, and of a slave a child, and of a creature that was worthless an acceptable being in His sight, know, I say, that He who did this is God ; and the reason why He did it was not any former desert of thine, nor any regard which He could have to the service which thou mightest afterwards perform, but it was solely of His own goodness and by the merit of our only Mediator Jesus Christ. . . . Acknowledge then thyself to be a debtor to Him and to His grace. Hearken to that which our Lord said to His beloved disciples, and through them to you, "You chose not Me, but I you."

'Lodge this, then, in thy heart, that as thou hadst thy *being* from God, without any cause to give glory to thyself, so also thou hast thy *wellbeing* from God, and that thou holdest both the one and the other for His glory.

'Carry, therefore, in thy heart and utter with thy tongue what St. Paul saith, "By the grace of God I am what I am." '

'Some think that because St. Paul said, "I would have men pray in every place," it is therefore unnecessary to pray in any particular place, but that it suffices to interlace our prayer with the rest of our works. And a good thing it is to pray in all places, but that will not suffice us if we would imitate Jesus Christ our Lord, and practise that which His saints have done in regard to prayer. For be thou well assured that no man will be able to pray with profit in *every* place unless first he have learnt to pray in a *particular* place and to employ some space of time therein.'

'"And the Lord said unto Moses, What is that in thine hand? And he said, A rod. And He said unto him, Cast it on the ground. And he cast it on the ground, and it became a serpent, and Moses fled from before it" (Exodus iv. 2, 3). What doth this teach us? but that as Moses fled from the serpent's fang, so do men naturally shrink from the touch and sight of suffering. But God commanded Moses to return towards that from which he had fled, and not only to return, but " to take it up in his hand ; " and he, obeying the voice of God, found in those hands of his no longer a serpent with poisonous fang, but a staff to uphold and support him. So is it with men who in the time of affliction obey the will of the Lord who hath sent it, and humbly " take hold " of the sorrow—it may be with trembling hands —to find comfort, support, and strength under it.'

THOUGHTS FOR CHRISTMAS.

'God loved us when He made us after His Image ; but a far greater work was it to make Himself after our image. He abases Himself to us, that He may exalt us to Himself.'

'Provide a cradle wherein you may rock the Infant Christ to rest. Yea, take care to nurse Him *in your heart*, that He suffer not from cold.'

'As soon as Christ is born in your heart, take ye care to nurse Him.'

.　　.　　.　　.　　.　　.

'He comes as a Stranger, and in great poverty. Give Him your heart to rest in, that He may say in the last day, " I was a stranger and ye took Me in." '

THOUGHTS FOR HOLY WEEK.

'There is no book so efficacious towards the instructing of a man in all virtue, and in abhorrence of all sin, as the PASSION OF THE SON OF GOD. . . .

'Employ then a part of each day in meditating on the Passion of our Lord, and in giving Him thanks for the benefits which are come to thee thereby, crying out from thine inmost heart, " I will never forget Thy benefits, for through them Thou hast given me life."

'Cast thyself upon thy knees . . . and do thou beseech

the Lord that He will send thee the light of the Holy
Spirit, to impart unto thee a tender compassionate feeling
for all that the Lord in the fulness of His love did suffer
for thee. Be very importunate in thy prayer. Then place
before thy mind's eye that mystery of the Passion on which
thou wouldest meditate. Count that He is *present*, and let
the eyes of thy soul rest at the foot of the Cross. Draw
near to Him, beholding with all reverence that which passeth
as though thou wast *present* at it. . . . Humble thyself
before Him with a simple kind of affection, as a poor little
child would do. For to love, is the end why we are to think
and meditate. . . .'

' The course then which thou shalt pursue is this :

' On Monday, think on the prayer of our Lord in His
agony ; how He was taken in the garden of Gethsemane,
and follow in thought that which took place in the house of
Annas and Caiaphas.

' On Tuesday, meditate on the accusations which were
presented against Him ; the processions from judge to judge,
and the cruel scourgings which He endured, bound to the
pillar.

' On Wednesday, think of Him crowned with thorns, and
with what scorn He was treated ; how they drew Him forth
arrayed in a scarlet robe, and with a reed in His hand, that
all the people might " Behold the Man."

' On Thursday, revert to that most holy mystery, when
the Son of God, with profound humility, washed the feet
of His disciples, and afterwards gave them His body and
blood for food of life, commanding both them and all, that
they should do the same in memory of Him.

' On Friday, think of our Lord before the Roman
governor, sentenced to death, bearing His cross upon His
back, and afterwards crucified upon it. Meditate upon all
which there passed till He commended His spirit into the
hands of His Father and died. . . .

' Behold now how much He loved thee !

'Come hither and gaze into the heart of thy Lord. If thou hadst the eyes of an eagle, here is whereon to gaze ; nay, even these could not enable thee to see in its intensity the burning flame of love which dwelt in His most holy soul. .

'They bound His hands with ropes, but understand thou that it was *within* that He was bound—bound by the meshes of mighty love, as immeasurably stronger than those ropes as chains of iron are beyond threads of flax.

'There stretched He out His arms to be nailed to the cross, in token that LOVE had opened wide His heart to all. The mighty beams of that love went forth from the centre of His heart to every man, past, present, and to come, offering up His life for the salvation of all.

'On Saturday, let thy thoughts rest on His sacred body . . taken down from the cross and laid in the sepulchre, and do thou in spirit accompany His soul to the place of departed spirits and be present at their joy.

'Let Sunday be set apart for the consideration of the Resurrection and the blessedness of those who have entered within the veil into heaven.

.   .   .   .   .   .

'If with quiet thinking of these things the Lord do give thee tears and compassion and other devout affections of mind, thou art to accept them *under this condition* . . . that no exterior signs, no outward show is made of what thou hast felt within. . . .

'For the end of thy meditation on the Passion is to be the imitation of Christ—*the fulfilling of the law of the Lord.* . . .

'Even as we read of Moses, who, having been forty days and forty nights on Mount Sinai in continual communion

with the Most High, when he descended from the mount to
converse with men spoke not of visions or of revelations
or of hidden mysteries ; *but there was a radiant light visible
on his face.   And in his hands he bore the two tables of stone.*

'If some little spark of the fire of love to Christ be
enkindled in our hearts, let us take great care that the wind
blow it not out, since it is but so little a spark.   Let us cover
it with the ashes of humility ; let us hold our peace and hide
it, and so we shall not lose it.   And let us daily add some
wood to it, as God commanded His priests to do, that the
fire might be kept alive on His altar, which signifies to us
the doing of good works ; and, above all things, we must
draw near to the True Fire, which will kindle and en-
flame us, which is Jesus Christ our Lord, in the Blessed
Sacrament.'

Juan de Avila, called the Apostle of Andalusia, was
born at Almadovar del Campo, in the diocese of Toledo,
on the Festival of the Epiphany, in the year 1500.   His
mother, like Hannah of old, had prayed for a child, and
after many years a son was given her—destined to be the
spiritual father of many saints in his native land.

He was the only child of his parents, who were devout
and wealthy, and from them he received his first religious
impressions.   From childhood he was remarkable for his
love of prayer and his self-denial.   At fourteen he was sent
to Salamanca to prepare himself for the legal profession ;
but he did not long pursue his forensic studies ; a vocation
higher than the law was ever present to his mind.   He
therefore returned to his parents and made known to them
his desire to dedicate his life to the service of God—a
desire which met with their full approval ; and permission
was given him to dwell in a small secluded corner of his
old home, and there commence a life of retirement and

devotion. Two years were thus passed when a Franciscan monk, struck with the profound reverence with which the boy knelt before the altar and received the Holy Sacrament, asked his history, and strongly advised his parents to send him to the University of Alcala, that he might study theology and prepare for the ecclesiastical state for which he was so manifestly destined. This counsel was adopted, and Juan commenced his studies at Alcala under Dominic del Soto, distinguished at that time for his commentaries on St. Thomas Aquinas.[1]

When Avila left college both his parents had been removed by death, and he immediately gave up all his patrimony to charitable purposes, and entered Holy Orders. His life was one of entire consecration to God, ever dying to his own will, and seeking to follow the law of Christ. From three to five o'clock every morning he was engaged in prayer and meditation, and two more hours were thus passed before he lay down to rest at night.

This was the secret of that serenity for which he was so remarkable. Juan's great desire was to go out as a missionary to America, and to preach the glad tidings of the

---

[1] Dominic del Soto became the confessor of the Emperor Charles V. He was of great authority at the Council of Trent, but his highest honour is that he is said to have been the *first* writer who condemned the African slave trade. In a lecture delivered at Salamanca, he says : 'It is affirmed that the unhappy Ethiopians are by fraud or force carried away and sold as slaves. If this is true, neither those who have taken them, nor those who purchased them, nor those who hold them in bondage, can ever have a quiet conscience till they emancipate them, even if no compensation should be obtained.' In the words of Sir Arthur Helps, 'The *re*-discovery of America by Columbus and the introduction of slavery may be said to go together.' The native Indians, exterminated by the cruelties inflicted on them by their Spanish conquerors, were replaced by unhappy Africans kidnapped from their homes, whose cause was thus nobly espoused by Del Soto, and by the devoted missionary Las Casas.

Gospel to the unhappy Indians.   The cry, 'Come over and help us,' which had stirred the soul of the great Apostle of the Gentiles, struck a chord of compassion in the heart of Juan ; but his archbishop refused to let him depart, and Andalusia—not America—was to be the scene of his missionary labours.

He had great facility of utterance, and his power of touching the hearts of his hearers when he preached was such that he seemed as one inspired.   A young priest on one occasion asked him by what means he could learn to preach with power, to which Avila replied, 'There is no other way, but ardent love of God.'

He was ever distrustful of himself and of his own abilities ; but he unceasingly prayed for the gift of the Spirit, that he might preach Christ to men, fully and faithfully.

On the day consecrated to the Magdalen, Juan was ordered to preach for the first time, in the cathedral of Seville, before his archbishop.   He had no sooner ascended the pulpit, and beheld the vast crowd of people standing below gazing up at him, than he became so confused and abashed that, for a few moments, all power of utterance forsook him.   He did not venture to lift his eyes again towards his hearers, but fixed them on the Crucifix before him, and silently prayed the Lord, in remembrance of His Shame and Humiliation when denuded, to succour His poor servant in this distress and perplexity, and to accord him the grace of one soul that day.

Immediately all fear left him, and he preached with so much unction that his auditors were filled with admiration of his eloquence.

Thus his career as a great preacher opened, and he soon became famous, not only as a preacher, but as a director of the conscience.

He had an insatiable thirst for the salvation of souls, and he never entered the pulpit without praying that the Life-giving Spirit would bring the words uttered home to the hearts of his hearers.

Men felt, as they listened to him, that their souls were precious in his sight, that he had a still and secret power, an anointing from the Holy One, which gave to his words an indescribable warmth and fervour, and marvellous were the conversions which resulted from his preaching.

His sermons were followed up by spiritual letters to his converts—letters which have been translated into many languages, and which have ever been regarded as models of spiritual guidance. If at any time one of his spiritual children relapsed into sin, it was to Avila as though he himself had fallen. He humbled and afflicted himself, and ' wept with the angels ' over him for whom Christ had died, and who had thus dishonoured his Lord afresh.

When he rebuked, it was never with harshness, always with tenderness and compassion, out of the abundance of a heart filled with gentleness and humility. It was said ' that he had a separate heart for each of those he loved, so that each one believed himself to be the best beloved.'

Juan de Dios, Francis Borgia, Teresa de Avila, and Luis de Granada regarded him as their spiritual father, and sat at his feet for instruction in the Divine Life. He enjoined meditation on the Passion as the sure way to attain a life of union with the Lord ; and it was his custom to keep especially sacred the night of Thursday and the Friday in each week, in remembrance of the midnight agony in the Olive Garden and the Cross on Calvary.

It was a sermon preached by Avila in the cathedral of Granada, on the death of the Empress Isabella, wife of Charles V., which led Francis Borgia to lay open to him his conscience, smitten and stirred with emotion by one look at the ravages of death. Francis Borgia, Duke of Gandia, was 'the star and pride of the Spanish nobility.' He was nearly related to the royal houses of Spain and Portugal, and was the trusty friend and favourite of the Emperor Charles V. He was Master of the Horse to the Empress Isabella, and on her death the duty devolved upon him of attending the body of his royal mistress from Toledo, where she died, to the burial-place of the kings of Spain at Granada.

The coffin had then to be opened, that he might swear to the identity of the body before it was laid in the vault ; but the beautiful and well-known features were no longer to be recognised. Horror-stricken at the sight, he from that moment resolved to turn from earth to heaven, and his newly awakened soul found guidance and consolation from Juan de Avila.

A few years later, and Borgia withdrew from the world, and became Father Francis of the Company of Jesus.

The name of Avila was loved and revered throughout Spain, and known to the whole Christian world. His writings, however, did not escape the censure of the Inquisition, and in 1534 he was cast into prison at Seville. He had to appear before the tribunal and reply to questions respecting his faith and teaching. He was accused of having in his sermons 'shut the rich out of the kingdom of heaven' by his denunciations of their vices and luxury. He bore all with perfect equanimity, never losing his serenity.

When in prison he was visited by Luis de Granada, and revealed to him the consolations he had received during his incarceration. Fresh light on the mysteries of Redemption had been poured into his soul, and he seemed overflowing with joy, in the consciousness of a closer union with Christ

—a consciousness which gave him strength and courage for every trial.

He was at length set at liberty, but the Inquisitors forbade him to preach, still insisting that some of his views were erroneous.

When finally his orthodoxy was established and he was permitted to appear in the pulpit at Seville, so great was the enthusiasm and joy of the whole city, that trumpets were sounded in triumph by the people. Some years afterwards one of his books was actually prohibited, and placed on the 'Index;' nevertheless he was selected by the Holy Office to examine and report upon certain views put forth in a work by Teresa of Avila, a work which he approved, but which he admitted to be unsuited to the general reader, certain passages needing to be well weighed, and others to be explained.

Avila fully acknowledged the good which the devout soul might derive from visions and spiritual revelations; but he deemed that great discernment and caution were necessary, and that no one should *seek* them, as they were but too often perilous illusions suggested by pride and self-seeking, and should only be accepted in so far as they tended to spiritual edification, rendering the person more humble and more devout.

St. François de Sales, in his 'Vie Dévote,' recommends the writings of Avila as a help to devotion in these words: Read these works with as much attention as if a saint from heaven had sent them to you, to teach you the way, and encourage you in walking in it.'

Many of the extracts in this volume have been taken from his work entitled 'Audi, filia,' which was addressed to a young girl named Sancha de Carillo, the daughter of a Spanish grandee, Don Luis Fernandez de Cordova.

C

Appointed to be maid of honor, Sancha suddenly renounced the world, and entreated Juan de Avila to direct her.

In these letters his great object was to impress upon her that it was not distaste for worldly amusements which should be her constraining motive, but the love of God, and the heartfelt desire to consecrate herself to His service.

In a sermon which he preached in the cathedral—once the mosque—of Cordova, he chose for his text 2 Kings iv. 40 : 'There is death in the caldron, O man of God, there is death in it.' At the conclusion he addressed himself specially to anyone present who might be living in open sin, and in a voice full of pathos exclaimed, 'Poor unhappy one, death is in that caldron from whence thou drawest thy subsistence. Cast away from thee the poisonous food ; cast it away now and for ever for the love of Him who gave His life to save thy soul, for in it is death. And why will ye die ?'

This sermon touched so profoundly the heart of one kneeling there, that, filled with contrition, she at once resolved to break from the sinful connection which had for years bound her to a Spanish noble. Children, home, earthly prosperity — all were renounced in that solemn hour. She had heard the Divine call, and at whatever cost she would arise and go to Him who came to seek and to save her soul. Great difficulties presented themselves, and very hindrance was offered to prevent the execution of her design. But Avila was resolved not to leave this precious soul in peril. So violent, however, was the opposition, that he was forced at length to have recourse to the strong arm of the law, and being provided with an escort, he succeeded, in spite of menaces and resistance, in consigning his convert from Cordova to a place of security in Granada, where for thirty years she led an exemplary life, and passed away from earth to heaven in the fulness of joy and peace.

Juan de Avila endeavoured to raise the condition, both moral and intellectual, of the clergy ; for this purpose he established classes in the different towns of Andalusia for their instruction. He also founded a theological college at Baeza, the professors being all men whom he had trained. It grieved Juan to the heart to see the low estate to which the clergy had fallen, and he was shocked at the ease and indifference with which men took upon themselves the sacerdotal state. 'They seemed,' he says, 'altogether to lose sight of the solemn duties and responsibilities of the ecclesiastical life, and merely to look to the possible emoluments and advantages which it opened up to them.'

The honour and dignity of the priesthood for its own sake were utterly disregarded. 'What a fearful abuse,' he exclaims, 'to approach the altar of sacrifice with the dominant thought of material subsistence. . . . Assuredly it is far better for a man to embrace any other profession—to work in hospitals serving the sick, to teach in schools, or, in fact, gain a livelihood, working with your hands in any humble way, as many saints have done in time past—rather than have the effrontery and audacity to stretch forth the hand towards heavenly things for the sake of securing the earthly. Appreciate the honour of waiting upon the sick, be content to take the lowest place and remain there, unless by unmistakable signs the Holy Spirit makes it clear to your inmost soul that your elevation to the priesthood is distinctly for the glory of God.'

Avila studied the Bible with great diligence ; he knew by heart all the epistles of St. Paul. He advised preachers to follow the example of keen sportsmen, who, when about to fly the falcon, carefully avoid feeding him, that he may pursue his prey with greater eagerness and vivacity ; so should preachers enter the pulpit, hungering for souls to be won to Christ, which hunger of the soul can only be attained by prayer and abstinence.

Avila constantly visited the hospitals and schools, and would gather men together in public places and preach to them the Gospel.   His intercourse with young priests was most beneficial.   One of his most frequent injunctions to those who sought his counsel was this, ' Go to prayer rather to *hearken* than to speak.   Bend humbly and lovingly before God, *expecting.*'

His mode of preparation for the Holy Sacrament is thus described in a letter to a young priest.

' During the previous night let your inward ear hearken to the cry, " *The Bridegroom cometh.   Go ye out to meet Him.*" When any great earthly personage is about to visit you, consider with what care, what solicitude you prepare beforehand for his reception.   With what anxiety you study to receive him with all due marks of honour.   With how much greater reason should the thought of *this Guest*, who is of such infinite majesty, absorb our hearts.   He that cometh to us is adored by the angelic host.   He is the King of kings, and yet He deigns to call us His brethren.   As you lie upon your bed think what it is for a poor sinful creature of this earth to be admitted to familiar converse with his God.

' Call to remembrance St. Peter, who felt unworthy to be even in the same vessel with his Divine Lord.   Think of the centurion, who ventured not to come to the house where the Lord was,[1] and let these thoughts deepen your reverence and awe before approaching so great a majesty. Remember that the Holy Sacrament is as a reproduction of

[1] St. Luke vii. 7.

the life and death of the Saviour. It mirrors forth to us the work of the Son when—sent by His Father—He entered the Virgin's womb for the salvation of men. He comes now to apply to our souls afresh the remedy which He obtained for us by His cross and passion. Receive Him, then, with the same holy joy as the Virgin experienced at the Incarnation.

'At the conclusion of the Mass retire for a while, and render humble thanks to the Lord for the honour He has conferred upon you in deigning to enter within such an unworthy abode. Ask pardon for your imperfect preparation and reception, and pray Him to free you from all sin and to bestow upon you of His boundless love grace for grace.'

Avila's perfect serenity was most striking; however multifarious his occupations, however uncongenial the persons with whom his duties brought him in contact, he was ever serene. He seemed always as though he had just issued forth from a long and fervent prayer, and 'his very look,' it was said, 'was enough to edify men.' He refused all court favour and all church preferment. Paul III. wished to make him a cardinal, but, true to his early choice, he remained a missionary throughout his life. His last years were spent in great bodily suffering. When dying, the rector of his college approached him and said, 'What joy it must be to you to think of meeting the Saviour!' 'Ah! rather do I tremble,' replied the dying saint, 'at the thought of my sins.'

He asked for the last Sacrament, and, holding the crucifix in his hand, repeatedly kissed the wounded feet, and passed away with the name of his Lord and Master on his lips, and a visage, calm and serene, sealed with the seal of God's peace. Avila was buried in the church of the Jesuits at Montilla, in Andalusia, where his epitaph is to be seen.

LUIS DE GRANADA.

B. 1504.   D. 1582.

'To think only of self is egotism; to think first of others is charity.'

'Look at the young sparrows perched on the top of the belfry. As soon as the bells begin to ring, away they fly, terrified. The old sparrows, on the contrary, who, long accustomed to the sound, know by experience that it brings no harm to them, remain in their nooks, perfectly unconcerned. So is it with those who for a long period have been in the habit of idly listening to the sound of the Gospel. Accustomed, like the old sparrows, to these tones, they are no longer in the least moved by them. And so it comes to pass that this fatal habit bars the door to their reception of eternal salvation.'

'In illumining others, the torch consumes itself.
'Such is the image of a Christian.'

'He who hearkens to the evil speaker, sins not less than he who speaks.'

'Love thy friends *in* God, and thine enemies for the love of God.'

'As thou shouldest avoid speaking evil of another, so shouldest thou shun speaking good of thyself.'

'Patience under injuries is the touchstone of true humility.'

'If thou shrinkest from humiliation thou wilt never be humble.'

'Learn to thrust back the word ready to start to thy lips, if thou feelest that it causeth thy blood to mount ever so little.'

'It is impossible that the love of God should grow in us without an evident increase of love towards our neighbour, as both are from the same source, and are like two branches growing out of the same trunk.'

'Suffer God to rule thee, to direct thee, and to work in thee what pleaseth Him, and let thy hand be directed by His Hand, as a pen in the hand of a writer which resisteth not.'

'Do not demand in everything *why* God thus made this and that ; for this word *why* is the word of the serpent and the beginning of our destruction. Shut the eyes of Reason and open the eyes of Faith, for Faith is the instrument by which alone Divine things are to be contemplated and searched into.'

'Even as from the circumference of a circle there are many lines tending to the centre, so there are many ways by which Christ leadeth His people to Heaven, which is the common centre of every one's felicity.'

'"If any man sin, we have an Advocate with the Father, Jesus Christ the Righteous, and He is the Reconciliation for our sins, and not for ours only, but also for the sins of the whole world " (1 St. John ii.) Why, then, dost thou suffer doubt and distrust to hinder thee, o'ershadowed as thou art by His wings, and covered by the merits of so great an Intercessor? All the sins in the world, in comparison with the infinite merits of Christ, are but as light chaff cast into the fire. Why, then, dost thou discourage thyself, seeing that such a full, perfect, and sufficient satisfaction has been thus *freely* offered unto thee? Thou wilt say, Because I offend every day and every hour, neither do I ever entirely amend myself. Tell me, if Christ should daily suffer for thy sins which thou daily committest, would there be any reason that thou shouldest despair? Thou wilt answer, No. Therefore assuredly persuade thyself that *that Death* so long ago suffered for thee is no less efficacious than if it were daily offered, for the Apostle saith that by One Oblation once offered upon the Cross hath the Great High Priest cleansed and sanctified us for ever.'

'As fire removed from the furnace immediately goeth out, except care be taken to feed and maintain it by ofttimes adding wood, even so hath the fire of love to God the like need of fuel to nourish it in a world where it is, as it were, a stranger and a pilgrim. And the fuel wherewith this holy love must be kept alive is *meditation*—meditation on the benefits and blessings bestowed on us by Almighty God and on His perfections. For to meditate on any one of these things acts even as a fagot or firebrand, kindling the fire of love, and causing this holy flame to blaze up brightly within our hearts. Let us therefore be watchful in maintaining this fire, according to the word of Almighty God, "Upon mine altar" (which is the heart of the just man) "the fire shall ever be burning" (Lev. vi. 12). So that the words of the Psalmist may be fulfilled in us, "Whilst I was thus musing the fire kindled" (Ps. xxxix. 4), even the fire of Divine love.'

'One of the great miseries of man's heart is that it is so quickly inflamed by the things of this world, and so slowly kindled into warmth by the things appertaining to Almighty God. To the one it is as a perfectly dry reed, ready to blaze up in an instant, whilst to the other it is as green wood which cannot be set light to save with the greatest difficulty.'

'Keep thine heart with all diligence, for out of it are the issues of life.' 'As the intemperateness of the air doth put a lute or a harp out of tune, much more without doubt is the tenderness and sensitiveness of man's heart troubled for lesser cause. Even as the sight of the eyes is hurt by a small thing entering in, and the brightness of a mirror is dimmed and obscured by a little breath, so a much less hurt and a much lighter cause is sufficient to dim and dull the brightness of our heart, to darken the eyes of our soul, and to disturb, together with our devotion, all our good affections. Therefore we must endeavour with great diligence, and with all our strength, to keep carefully and safely a treasure so precious and which is so easily lost.'

'Even as our fleshly eyes cannot behold the stars, nor the beauty of heaven, when it is cloudy and overcast, so neither can the eyes of our souls contemplate the Eternal Light when they are obscured by the clouds and passions of this life.'

'As sweet perfume standing in an open vessel, having no cover, doth forthwith lose the sweetness and fragrance of the scent ; so the sweet and precious ointment of devotion doth lose all virtue and efficacy when the mouth is loosed, and the tongue doth lavish and superabound in religious talk. Therefore it is best to be silent, and if at any time it be needful to speak, yet speedily, like the dove, return into the ark, lest thou perish in the deluge of words.'

' As they that have the charge and keeping of a clock are wont every day to wind up the plummets, for they of their own proper motion do, by little and little, descend and draw towards the ground ; so they that desire to keep their souls upright and well ordered ought, at the least twice a day, to lift up the weights ; seeing that our wretched nature is so inclinable to things below, that it always endeavoureth to sink downwards. . . . He therefore that would always have the clock of his life well ordered and governed, must always have a special regard to wind up the plummets and weights of it.'

' A man without prayer and without spiritual exercise is

as Samson without his hair, so that he remaineth feeble and weak like other men, and is in great danger of falling into the hands of his soul's enemies.'

'If at any time thou dost stumble and fall, and, through weakness, dost faint, do not discourage thyself, nor cast away thy hope; but albeit thou fall a thousand times in a day, rise again, and be renewed a thousand times in a day; and in what place thy thread was broken, knit it together again, and go not back to the beginning.'

'As with a harp, we must be careful that the strings be neither stretched too tight nor loosened too slack (for then they are either broken or yield an inharmonious sound), so in regard to celestial music, it is necessary that the body be neither macerated by too much fasting, nor fatted by too much plenty; for both of these bring very much hurt to the exercise of devotion. For this cause God commanded in the old Law that *salt* should be sprinkled upon all the sacrifices, that He might teach us that none of our sacrifices, however great, are acceptable unto Him unless they be seasoned with salt—that is, *with the savour of discretion.*'

'I have lost, thou sayest, a son, a brother, a husband, the partner of my solitude, the staff of my old age, the comfort of my widowhood, my all! Without him I am as one at sea without a compass; and who can help me in this my sore distress, bereft of all?

'If thou hast confidence in thy Lord, if thou dost cling to Him, if thou dost implore His help, putting in Him all thy trust, He will be to thee a father, a brother, a sister, a husband. If Elkanah could say to Hannah, his wife, "Hannah, why weepest thou? Why is thy heart grieved? Am I not better to thee than ten sons?" (1 Sam. i. 8) with how much greater reason may not the Lord hold this language to the faithful, loving soul? For what may we not expect from Him who is the source of all blessings, the refuge and strength not only of widows, but of all the desolate, all the unhappy, all that walk in darkness and have no light ? '

'Learn from the mystery of the Pool of Bethesda that as only he who arose and went in speedily after the moving of the water received the blessing, so should those who have tasted the sweetness of divine things, whenever inwardly moved towards a spiritual colloquy, at once respond to the call of the Heavenly Bridegroom ; otherwise, by negligence and delay, they may altogether lose the proffered grace of a Divine Visitation. This we learn also from the Canticles, for when the Bride, after long delay, at length opened to the Bridegroom, who had knocked in vain at her door, she found Him not, she had opened to Him too late.'

'As oil has this especial quality among liquids, that it always rises to the surface, and claims the highest place ; so the love of Christ, the thought of Heaven, should dominate over all, should rise above all, and never yield its place.'

'The Creator has given such a property to the load-stone that iron, when rubbed by it, turns constantly towards the pole, where only it has full repose, and, when given another direction, is in continual agitation. So has He given to the human soul such a nature that it can only find rest when turned towards Himself, and, apart from Him, is ever troubled and disquieted, even though possessed of all earthly things.'

'God manifested to man His great love, not only under the law of grace and mercy, but also under the Mosaic law, at a time when love had less rule than fear. In proof of this, remember the name which He gives to that place which He chose as His dwelling. He called it not by the name of Tribunal, nor of Palace, nor of Throne. He called it the Mercy Seat . . . as if to take away from us all fear and distrust, and to draw us near to Him by the hope of mercy and pardon.'

' " Blessed are the pure in heart, for they shall see God."
What must be the Beatitude to which so great a reward is
promised ? What felicity so great as to behold the radiance
of the Divine beauty? If you would partake of this, seek
purity of heart as the end and aim of your life. This virtue
consists, not merely in keeping the soul free from the de-
filement of sin, but free also from earthly cravings, and
those impressions which are produced on the soul by carnal
thoughts. As then it is by the door of the senses that
these penetrate into the soul, it behoves him who would
keep jealous guard over the purity of his heart to watch
with vigilance over the senses, for, should he allow them to
wander on all objects around, the purity of his soul will
assuredly receive some taint, some stain. He could not do
better than to imitate the sportsman, who covers with a
hood the head of the falcon which he holds on his wrist,
that it may not be excited by the sight of some bird or other
object. By this means the sportsman prevents its struggling
and attempting to take flight ; thus it is made subservient to
his will, and is only permitted to fly when he deems it fit.'

———◦◇◦———

Twelve years before the birth of Luis, Granada—the
ast stronghold of the Moors, the glorious city of ' running
rivers and fountains '—had surrendered after a long siege to
the Catholic sovereigns Ferdinand and Isabella.

Boabdil, El Zogobi (the luckless one), the last Moorish
king, with his band of warriors left the city through the
gateway of Los Siete Suelos[1] as distant shouts of triumph
announced that the Christian hosts had entered the Alhambra by the grand gateway of the Torre de Justicia.

An inscription on the highest tower of the citadel marks
the date of this event—January 2, 1492. On the morning of

---

[1] This gateway of Los Siete Suelos (or the Seven Stories) has been
closed ever since.

that day Mendoza, the Cardinal Primate of Spain, followed by a glittering train of knights, ascended to the Torre de la Vela and planted upon its battlements a silver cross, in token that Granada was now a Christian city, and that the infidel power in Spain was for ever overthrown.

As the symbol of Christian faith rose to view, gleaming in the cloudless sky, the whole Spanish army, encamped in the plains below, bent the knee before the sacred emblem, and with one voice chanted the solemn anthem, 'Te Deum Laudamus.' But no deeds of Christian mercy marked the entrance of the conquerors into the captured city. The solemn engagement made by Ferdinand and Isabella that 'no Moor should be forced to embrace the Christian religion against his will' was at once set aside as 'incompatible with the glory and security of the Christian community.' [1] Baptism or exile was the alternative offered alike to Jew and Moslem, and thousands left houses and lands and exchanged wealth for penury rather than forsake the faith of their fathers.

Among those who watched that silver cross as it slowly rose above the towers of the Alhambra was Christopher Columbus, who, before another year had passed, gave a new world to Castile and Leon.

In this fair city of Granada, Luis, the great Dominican preacher, was born. His family name was Sarras, but he adopted in its stead that of his birthplace, by which he is commonly known. He is described by Ticknor as among the most prominent of the Spanish mystics.[2] His father died when Luis was five years old, leaving his widow in great poverty. She earned a scanty living as laundress to a Dominican convent ; but her means often failed, and she

---

[1] See *British and Foreign Review*, No. 15, 1839.
[2] See *History of Spanish Literature*.

had to depend upon the alms given her by the friars. Luis was sent to school, and in the courts of the beautiful Alhambra he and his schoolfellows were wont to play. On one occasion their sport ended in rude rough blows, and the shouts of the boy combatants reached the ears of the Spanish governor, the Count de Tendilla, the first alcaide of the Alhambra, who sharply rebuked them for their noisy violence. Luis, however, came boldly forward to justify his conduct, and defended himself with so much ability that the Count de Tendilla, struck with the boy's language and manner, ordered that inquiries should be made as to his history, and finally appointed him page to his young son, with whom he was henceforth educated. His natural eloquence, fostered by instruction, quickly developed into great oratorical powers. Theology was his favourite study, and it is said that when a mere lad he would gather the youth of Granada together and preach to them in the open air. As he grew in years so there grew within him an intense desire to enter the ecclesiastical state, but no other opening presenting itself, he became an acolyte in the royal chapel of Granada.

The daily services of the Church were his delight. He resolved to dedicate himself wholly to God, and when nineteen he entered the Dominican convent of Santa Cruz.

The thought of his mother was ever present to him, and he asked permission from his superior to share with her the small portion of food allotted to himself. His request was granted, and his mother was given the half of the daily meal of her son without ever knowing to whom she owed it. Throughout his life his filial love and veneration remained unchanged.

From Santa Cruz, Luis was admitted to the college of San Gregorio, at Valladolid, where his talents had procured him a fellowship. On his return to Granada he commenced his duties as a preacher. He diligently prepared himself by prayer and the study of the Scriptures. He also made numerous extracts from the writings of the Fathers of the Church and from classical authors, whose words he frequently quoted in his discourses. Crowds thronged to listen to him, and so powerfully were the consciences of his hearers affected, that we are told 'those who came to hear went home to pray.'

Pure, humble, holy in life, his example gave additional force to his words, and before long a moral reformation was effected in his convent.

He was appointed by the general of the Dominicans prior of the convent of Scala Cœli, a deserted building high up in the rugged mountains above Cordova and supposed to be haunted by evil spirits. Nothing could exceed the dreariness and loneliness of the place, but Granada was in no way discouraged. To restore a convent once renowned for its sanctity was a task worthy of his zeal. He chose for his fellow-workers men earnest as himself, and animated with the same desire of re-establishing this decayed monastery and bringing glory to God by preaching the Gospel to the mountaineers dwelling in the wild region around. Success crowned their efforts, and the fame of Scala Cœli revived.

Luis de Granada at times descended to Cordova, preaching in the wondrous mosque which had now become a Christian sanctuary. On one of these occasions he became known to Juan de Avila, whose opinion was asked respecting the sermon delivered by Granada. Granada waited anxiously his judgment. For some time Avila made no reply. At length he spoke : 'No sermon contents me where Christ crucified is not preached.'

The words made deep impression on Granada, and from
that day forth he chose Avila as his spiritual director and
guide.   Avila's advice to him was, '*Stint thyself.*'   Luis did
not understand what these words implied, and asked for
further explanation.   Avila replied, 'Hunger and thirst *only*
for the conversion of souls.   Let there be no hungering for
the praise of men.   Let self-love be starved, then will God
give thee plenteous result.'

Some years afterwards Granada said to Avila, before
many witnesses, 'I owe more to you and to your counsel
than to years of study, and therefore I acknowledge you
before all men to be my master.'   Avila stopped him.   'The
true master is God, unto whom all honour is due.'

After eight years spent at Scala Cœli, Granada was removed to Badajoz to assist in the foundation of a Dominican convent, and here he composed his 'Sinners' Guide,' a
work which he wrote after perusing Alcantara's 'Golden
Book.'   For fourteen years the 'Sinners' Guide' was prohibited by the Inquisition, and Granada himself was brought
under suspicion of heresy.   The book nevertheless made
its way throughout Spain, and was translated into every
European language.[1]

To avoid further molestation, Granada prudently withdrew from his native country.   He became head of the
Dominican order, or Order of Preaching Monks, in Portugal,
where he enjoyed the protection and friendship of Queen
Catherine, sister of the Emperor Charles V., who made him
her confessor.   She was most desirous of conferring upon

---

[1] The *Guide for Sinners* was placed on the ' Index Expurgatorius '
the very year after it was published, but after fourteen years' prohibition
the Holy Office withdrew the censure, and proclaimed special indulgences to whomsoever should read a chapter of the once condemned
work.

him the archbishopric of Braga, but Luis steadily refused the offer.

The latter part of his life was spent at Lisbon, in the convent of St. Dominic, devoting himself to the reformation of his order, with occasional visits to a lonely monastery where he retired for solitude and meditation.

When at Lisbon he preached frequently before the court. He was ready at all times to receive those who came to him for comfort or for counsel, but other visitors were courteously dismissed. His practice was to rise at four in the morning, and devote two hours to mental prayer. He never missed the daily celebration, and enjoined this rule upon others as the greatest spiritual help and sustenance. His whole life may be said to have been one long prayer, so constant was his converse with his Lord and Master in the midst of his varied occupations. His sight had always been weak, and after a night spent in preparation of a sermon to be preached on the following day, he suddenly became blind of one eye. He preached, notwithstanding, with his usual unction as though nothing had occurred to disturb him.

When he felt that his end was near, he begged to be left for a while perfectly alone. He afterwards desired that the Passion of our Lord should be read to him before receiving the last Sacrament.

He died in the same year as St. Teresa.

The first Spanish translation of the 'Imitation of Christ' was made by Luis de Granada, and his 'Meditation on Prayer' was a favourite book of Charles V. at Yuste.

SANTA TERESA DE JESUS DE AVILA.

B. 1515.   D. 1582.

'The love of God has this advantage over all other loves, viz. that in loving Him *we are sure that He loves us.*'

'Do all things as if you verily saw God Himself present before you; for in this way the soul makes rapid progress.'

'Try never to dwell on the imperfections of others, but on *their* virtues and *your own* imperfections.'

'Let that soul never give up prayer which has once begun it. Be the life ever so sinful, prayer is the way to amend it; therefore let not Satan tempt the soul to cease from it on pretence of humility, but let us rather believe His word who has said, that if we truly repent and resolve to lead a new life, He will receive us again into His favour, and give us fresh grace, yea, even greater grace, it may be, if our repentance be deep and earnest.'

'The love and the fear of God are like two strong fortresses, from whence we wage war against the world and the devil.'

'Let us learn to contradict our own will.'

'To repeat the Lord's Prayer well, we must remain near the Divine Master, who will teach it us.'

'Believe me, you gain much more by *leisurely* saying one sentence of the Lord's Prayer, than by frequently repeating the whole hurriedly, without letting it sink in.'

'It is an admirable custom to shut the eyes in prayer; it is *forcing* ourselves not to behold things outward.'

'Be gentle to all, and to yourself severe.'

'Since you find words to speak to others, why should you lack them to speak to God? Accustom yourself to speak openly to Him, and words will not be wanting. If we cease for a long period from converse with a person, we feel a sort of estrangement, and an ignorance as to *how* we should speak. It almost seems at last as if we did not know the person, even though he be a near relation ; for kindred and friendship are soon lost sight of for want of communion and intercourse.'

'Great, indeed, is the mercy of our God ! What friend shall we find so patient ? When a breach once takes place between two intimate friends, it is never entirely forgotten. They are never again such trustful friends as they were before. But how many times have we broken our friendship with God ; and what years has He not waited for us to turn and repent ! '

'Believe firmly in the love which the Lord has for you, for it is no small happiness and encouragement to a scholar to know that his master loves him.'

'The devil tries to make us think we have humility when in reality he is trying to make us distrust God. When you find yourself discouraged and cast down, avoid, as much as possible, dwelling on your own sinfulness and misery, and meditate rather on His great mercy, on the love He bears you, and on all He suffered for you.'

'If you hear anyone much praised, rejoice more at this than if you yourself were praised. This, indeed, should not be difficult, for, where there is true humility, praise gives pain.'

'Fix your eyes on your Crucified Lord, and everything will seem easy to you.'

'If you prick a living person with a needle, however slightly, is it not felt ? or with a thorn, however small it may be, does it not give pain ? So the soul, if it be not dead, but living unto God, must, by His grace, feel grieved

for anything said or done, however small, which is contrary
to Christian profession.'

'It is a dangerous peace, and beware of it when anyone
commits the same fault again and again, *esteeming it as nothing*, having no remorse of conscience, and making no
attempt to correct it.'

'Suffer not a fault to take root, for then it will be eradi-
cated with much difficulty, and it may even happen that
from it may spring many suckers. If we were to water
every day a noxious plant in our garden, it would grow so
large that, after a time, it would require a spade or mattock
to dig it up. Such is the result, also, when we daily commit
the same fault, however little it may be, without attempting
to correct it. If, on the contrary, it be checked at once,
the work will be easy.'

'Let not those who have been called to an active life in
Christ's service envy those who have been led to a life of
contemplation. . . . Remember that there must be some to
wait at His table, and let those account themselves happy
who are called to serve with Martha. For what can anyone
desire more than to resemble that blessed woman, who we
may believe often entertained the Lord in her house. Had
she been like blessed Mary—always absorbed in devotion—
there would have been no one to provide food for the Divine
Guest.'

'True humility is chiefly shown in being ready and con-
tented to do whatsoever the Lord shall be pleased to ap-
point, ever counting ourselves as unworthy to be called His
servants.'

'Consider what St. Augustine says, viz. " That he sought
God in many places, and came at last to find Him in himself." Do you think that it is but of little importance to
recognise this truth ; to know that we need not mount to

heaven to speak with our Eternal Father? nor need we
speak aloud, for, however low our voice, He is so near that
He will hear us. Neither do we require wings to fly and
seek Him, for we have but to be still and to quiet ourselves
to behold Him *within* ourselves. . . . Let us not then slight
so gracious a Guest, but reflect how much it concerns us to
recognise this great truth, viz. that *God dwells within* us,
and that there we should dwell with Him. . . . It is in this
recollectedness that the soul gathers together or *re-collects* all
its faculties, and, entering within itself, has communion with
the Divine Lord.'

'Figure to yourself that *within you* there is a palace . . .
and that in this palace the Great King dwells who has
been pleased to become your Guest, and that He sits there
on a throne of infinite value, which is your *heart.*
'This may at first sound foolish or extravagant, yet it
may be of great help to make us understand that there is
within us something beyond comparison more precious than
all which we see outwardly.
'If we did but remember that we have within us such a
Guest, it would be impossible for us to be so fond of the
things of this world, for we should feel how trivial and base
they are in comparison with those treasures we possess
within.
'All this was at one time obscure to me. I knew well
that I had a soul ; but I understood not the dignity of this
soul, nor knew Who dwelt within it ; because my eyes being
blinded by the vanities of this life, I was prevented from
seeing Him. Had I then known, as I do now, that in this
palace of my soul so great a King dwells, I should not have
neglected Him and left Him so often, but should have
stayed with Him, and have been more anxious to prepare
Him a fit dwelling. . . . The great point lies in our giving
up this palace to Him as His own with a full and perfect
surrender, that He may abide there, and place or take away
from thence whatsoever He pleases—as it is His own. . . .

Refuse it not to Him, for He will not *force* our will, He
will only take what we give Him. But He gives not Himself *entirely* to us till we thus give ourselves up *entirely* to
Him. And He only works thoroughly within that soul
which offers no hindrance, *but is wholly His.* But if, on the
contrary, we crowd this palace of the soul with other guests,
with rabble and with rubbish, what room is there for the
Lord to enter in ?

'It is very useful for us to remember that we have a
Guest to entertain *within us* ; and that we should be conscious of His presence and abide with Him ; seeing Him
with the inward eye and speaking to Him ; never turning
our backs upon Him ; which is, methinks, what we do
when we remain on our knees discoursing to all appearance
with our Divine Lord, whilst at the same time we let our
thoughts run on a thousand vanities. All this evil arises
from our not properly apprehending that *He is near us ;
within us.*'

'By little and little obtain the mastery over your own
selves. Lose not the spirit of *recollectedness* for mere trifles,
but learn to recall your senses within you. When about to
pray, remind yourself that you are about to hold converse
with One within you. Wait and listen that you may hear
what the Lord God will say unto you ; and as you hearken,
remember that you are waiting to hear One who speaks not
audibly but to the inmost soul.

.   .   .   .

'If possible let this holy exercise be frequent in the
course of the day ; but if this cannot be, at least let it be a
daily devotion and practice. When you have accustomed
yourself to it, you will gradually find yourself gaining greatly
from it ; and when our Lord shall have granted unto you
the grace of holy fellowship, you will find that you would
not exchange it for any earthly treasure.'

'Have no fear of death, but look upon it as a sweet trance.'

'Let nothing disturb you.
Let nothing alarm you.
All things pass away.
God is unchangeable.
Patience gains everything.
He who possesses God lacks nothing.
God alone is All-sufficient.' [1]

In the mediæval city of Avila, a city of Old Castile, founded in 1088, shut in from the outer world by granite walls and towers of vast strength and height, Teresa, the great Spanish saint of the sixteenth century, first saw the light.

In a book filled with family memorials in the handwriting of her father, Don Alfonso Sanchez de Cepeda, the day of the birth of Teresa of Avila is thus carefully noted :

'This day, Wednesday, March 28, 1515, my daughter Teresa was born, about half-past five in the morning, at the first streak of dawn.'

The bells of the different churches in the old city were sounding the first Angelus, but one rung on that day with a longer and more joyous peal than the rest. It was the bell of the Carmelite Monastery of the Incarnation, which was but just completed, and March 28 had been appointed for the inauguration of the Chapel. A celebration of the Holy Sacrament was announced by this glad peal, but it likewise unconsciously proclaimed the birth of one destined to be the great Saint and Reformer of the Carmelite Order. [2]

[1] St. Teresa carried these words in her breviary as her ' signet.'
[2] See *Histoire de Ste. Thérèse d'après les Bollandistes.*

A memorable era had already commenced.

The discovery of the art of printing in the preceding century had brought forth treasures which had long lain hidden in manuscript. Cardinal Ximenes, ever eager to advance learning among his countrymen, had in 1514 (the year before Teresa's birth) given to Spain a polyglot Bible in the Hebrew, Greek, Chaldee, and Latin text, known as the ' Complutensium '[1]—a work through which an immense impulse was imparted to Biblical research ; and when the tutelar saint of Spain was but two years old, Martin Luther, in his righteous indignation at the sale of indulgences, affixed his theses to the gate of the cathedral of Wittemberg, and the contest began which rent asunder the unity of the Latin Church.

The father of Teresa, Alfonso Sanchez de Cepeda, was descended both on his father's and his mother's side from old and distinguished Castilian families, and his life was worthy of his high. lineage. He married twice. The early death of his first wife left him a widower with three children. He wedded secondly Beatrix Davila de Ahumada, the mother of Teresa and eight other children.[2]

Teresa describes her father as truthful, virtuous, and full of compassion, and her mother as gentle, retiring, and unconscious of her great beauty. Their home was one of peace, undisturbed by worldly intercourse. Such influence could not be without effect on the minds of their children. ' All except myself' (says Teresa in her humility) 'resembled our parents ; ' but in truth in early childhood none were affected in the same degree as herself by the hallowing

---

[1] Spain was thus possessed of an edition of the New Testament in the original Greek two years before the Greek Testament of Erasmus made all Europe ring with his fame.

[2] Teresa adopted the surname of her mother.

influence which surrounded them. The child loved to listen to her mother's prayers, and to her brother Rodriguez she imparted some of her religious fervour. They read together the lives of the saints, and the cruel martyrdoms they endured for the love of Christ so excited the imagination of the two children that they resolved, when Teresa was but seven years old, to steal forth on a mission to convert the Moors or die in the attempt. It was an attempt at which the world may smile, but, as it has been well said, 'it was a fit beginning for a life of passionate devotion.' With little hands outstretched to grasp the martyr's palm they left their home together, and had made their way beyond the old gates of Avila, when they were met by their uncle as he was returning to the city, and the disappointed missionaries were conducted home.

Foiled in their great enterprise, the two children fell back upon the hermit life, and made themselves cells for devotion in their father's orchard. This childish enthusiasm in Teresa's case was not of long duration. As she grew older her religious zeal waxed faint. When she was thirteen her mother died, and a time of peril followed for the motherless girl. As she advanced to womanhood she became conscious of the beauty she had inherited, and was not indifferent to the admiration she excited. Her vivacity and natural eloquence added to her charm ; her sprightliness made her a delightful companion, and the desire to shine in the society of her companions became a ruling passion. She speaks with humiliation of this period of her life—of her vanity and selfishness. The lives of the saints—her early study—no longer interested her ; exciting romances, stories of chivalry, were her delight, and to this baneful reading she traces 'the beginning of her lukewarmness in all good desires.'

Three years passed away without much change in Teresa : her father had not failed to observe with pain that his favourite child turned away from books of devotion and went less frequently to church. He spoke to her on the subject with some severity, but Teresa would fly into his arms with endearing caresses and excuses which he was only too ready to accept.

But the marriage of an elder sister led to a change in Teresa's life. She was placed by her father in a convent at Avila under the care of pious Augustinian nuns. She was the joy and sunbeam of her father's home, and it was a hard sacrifice to separate her from himself, but he felt that it was needful for his child's welfare now that she was deprived of the watchful eye of her sister. Convent life seemed at first very dreary to Teresa. The discipline, slight as it was, chafed and wearied a nature impatient of restraint ; but gradually the habits and feelings of her earlier years revived, and she grew reconciled to the monotony and silence of the cloister, but without any thoughts as yet of becoming a nun.

She had been in the convent about eighteen months when a severe illness caused her removal to her father's house. To while away the tedious hours she had again recourse to devotional reading, and she became impressed by the works of the Fathers of the Church. The words of St. Jerome, St. Gregory, and St. Augustine sank deep into her mind. It chanced that a little picture was hung in her room which represented our Lord and the woman of Samaria at the well. This picture greatly affected Teresa, and before she lay down at night she would look at it and say with the poor sinner, ' Domine, da mihi hanc aquam '— a prayer which she afterwards used through life. By degrees her heart warmed and responded to the touch of

Divine grace ; but, remembering the past, and conscious of her own weakness, she resolved to flee from the temptations of the world and take refuge in the Carmelite Monastery of the Incarnation. To aid her in this design, Teresa had within the walls of the monastery a friend—Juana Suarez— whose prayers had been continually directed to this end. She was not yet nineteen, and when she made known her wishes to her father he refused his consent. Nothing daunted, she resolved again to steal away from her home as she had done once before. It was not without a pang that she left her father, and in company with one of her brothers went forth at an early hour on All Souls' Day, November 2, 1533, and presented herself at the gate of the monastery which stood outside the city walls. She was received by the prioress and her friend Juana, and taking leave of her brother, she was at once admitted into the chapel of the Incarnation. It was the day of commemoration of the dead, and the solemn requiem was sounding as Teresa bade fare- well to the world, and, with hair shorn and clothed in the dress of a novice, took the lowest place among her future companions. When informed of her flight, her father gave an unwilling consent to the step she had taken.

The year of her novitiate was on the whole a happy one ; but she was accustomed to praise, and there were times when a want of response or a cold look from her com- panions would chill her, and then came a passionate yearn- ing for home affections and sympathy—a longing to be again petted and cherished as she had been in her father's house. But if the thought arose, 'Should she withdraw from conventual life and return to home duties?' she thrust it aside. She had put her hand to the plough, and she resolved not to look back.[1]

[1] See *Histoire de Ste. Thérèse.*

She had reached her twentieth year when she made her formal profession as a nun. All the chief families of Avila crowded to the monastery to witness the ceremony, and her father, who had reluctantly yielded up his favourite child to the cloister, came to see her consummate the act of self-immolation.

But their separation at this time was not for long. Teresa's health soon began to fail, and symptoms of paralysis forced her to leave the monastery and return home, where for three years she led a life of suffering.

It was during this period that she commenced that method of mental prayer with which her name became associated, and which she describes as 'shutting herself up within herself.'

Her health was at length re-established, and in 1539 she went back to her convent. But with the return of youthful strength and vigour of body came spiritual decay, and the conventual life as then constituted was little calculated to raise her in heart and mind. Never were religious houses in a more neglected condition. They were indeed only religious in name. No rules were prescribed for guidance and help in the spiritual life; no works of mercy or benevolence were enjoined, and beyond the formal offices no occupation was provided for the nuns, who, instead of renouncing the world for a life of usefulness and devotion, had only exchanged their home life with its duties and occupations for a life of idleness, ease, and frivolity. It was not indeed wholly without distraction from the outer world. When the daily offices were duly said, visitors were admitted to the convent. With the visitors came the brothers and other relations of the nuns, and these social gatherings, which must have been their chief resource and recreation, became the occasion for idle gossip and scandal. Teresa's ready wit and liveliness made her the centre of these meetings, but she soon felt that this talk of the lips brought penury to the soul, and so far from attaining to that separation from the world and complete consecration of spirit for which she had fled from her home, she found that 'the garden of her soul had ceased to be inclosed,'[1] and that every passer-by was permitted to pluck the fruit. As her love waxed cold, secret prayer was neglected, and meditation was relinquished. In the bitterness of her soul she says, 'On the one side God called me, on the other the world drew me, and *I followed the world.*' Her life became 'a daily heart-break and humiliation, a perpetual falling, and rising to fall again.' She strove to reconcile God and the world, and her spirit grew restless and dissatisfied in the attempt.

In this state she listened to the suggestions of the great enemy of souls, and gave up secret prayer altogether, which she only resumed after the death of her father. She had nursed him through his last illness, which aroused her to higher thoughts, and she resolved to resume mental prayer. She did so, but she could not make up her mind to forsake *all* that held her back and which her conscience condemned. She tried to pray, but the light of God's countenance seemed hidden from her; she felt as though shut out from the Divine Presence. Thus was she for fourteen years, without consolation, straitened and desolate within herself. But that which she had striven for in vain in her own strength, she obtained by one ray of light from on high. 'The Lord whom she sought came suddenly to His temple,' revealing to her inmost soul His infinite love. We are told that during Lent 1555, when she was forty years old, she one day withdrew, sad and weary in spirit, to a small oratory, where she was wont to resort. A sacred

[1] Canticles iv. 12.

picture had recently been placed there without her knowledge. It represented Christ bound to a column and scourged.[1] As she gazed on the stricken form, her heart was moved within her, and the thought of how little return she had made for such love, touched her to the quick. With a sudden pang of grief she threw herself on the ground and burst into tears, crying aloud, 'O my Lord, I will not let Thee go except Thou bless me.' It was the awakening of her soul to a recognition of her sinfulness before God, and of the depth of Divine love. Soon after this 'The Confessions of St. Augustine' fell into her hands. She had never met with this book, and in her 'Life' she tells us that she doubted not that it was given her at this time to fulfil some special purpose of God. As she read, she seemed to see herself. It was a revelation to her of her own heart, with all its infirmities and errors; and when she came to the account of Augustine's conversion, it was as if she too heard the voice of the Lord speaking to her innermost soul and opening to her a new and higher calling. Hitherto she had counted her life as her own; now she surrendered her whole being to God. She had passed from death unto life, and the words of the Bride in the Canticles were ever sounding on her inward ear, 'My Beloved is mine, and I am His.'[2]

Day by day the love enkindled within her soul blazed with intenser, purer light. She resumed the old method of prayer, '*shutting herself up within herself*;' but with it came a power and vitality hitherto unknown. From henceforth a new phase commenced in her existence—an epoch of

---

[1] At the present day there is upon the altar of the chapel at Avila an ivory figure representing Christ scourged, which belonged to Teresa.

[2] See *Histoire de Ste. Thérèse.*

transition. She passed insensibly from the outer court of devotion and entered within the veil.

Her prayers were now communings with the Lord, and she had a distinct personal consciousness of union with Him. She loved to dwell on the mysteries of the Passion, especially on His desertion and betrayal. She would meditate on His agony in the olive garden, placing herself in spirit beside Him, tarrying with Him in His loneliness, gazing upon Him in His sorrow. She beheld Him, she tells us, not with the eyes of the flesh, but by an act of living faith as present to her soul. To abide evermore in His presence was her one great object, and she teaches us that 'the soul which thus looks constantly on Him becomes inflamed with His love, ever turning to Him for counsel, crying to Him in time of need, complaining to Him in time of sorrow, and rejoicing with Him in time of joy.'

Visions and revelations of the unseen were accorded to her, but these she regarded at first with fear and misgiving. She dreaded to become the victim of delusions like Magdalen of the Cross, the nun of Cordova, whose confessions had lately scandalised the Church.[1]

Teresa herself fully believed that the special graces vouchsafed to her in prayer were from above; but doubtful of the light and experience she possessed, she desired earnestly to be guided by the judgment of others better skilled than herself in the mysteries of the spiritual life.

She had recourse to Gaspar Daza, a learned priest, who came at her request to the monastery, accompanied by an old and devout friend of Teresa's family, Don Francisco de Salcedo. Teresa revealed to them her spiritual state, and described her experiences in prayer.

The result of the interview was adverse to her hope, and

[1] See *Mystiques espagnols* (Rousselot).

the decision a painful one.   Both men were convinced that, so far from being special graces, her experiences were the work of the Evil One, and mental prayer was by their decision to be put aside.

Teresa's anguish was extreme.   She remembered how her soul had languished in former years, when she had relinquished mental prayer, and what consolations she had since received on returning to her old method.   Was she now to be debarred from this spiritual comfort?   Were the experiences she had thought so blessed in very truth a snare of the devil?   In her distress she called to her help a Jesuit father, a course recommended to her by Don Francisco.   This Jesuit was Father Padranos.   He had been lately sent on a mission to Avila by Francis Borgia— a name which inspired Teresa with confidence.   The Padre received his new penitent gravely, but kindly.   To him she made a full confession, revealing to him all that weighed upon her heart.   He at once understood the character with which he had to deal.   Her extreme humility, her truthfulness and candour, her tenderness of heart, and ardent faith —these were forthwith apparent to him, but beyond these were supernatural gifts, marvels of grace bestowed upon her by God, which filled him with joy and amazement. Padranos had come to the monastery forewarned by Don Francisco, and anxious as to her state ; he came thinking to deliver a poor visionary from Satan's wiles, and he found himself in the presence of a saint.[1]

Teresa was greatly reassured by his consoling words ; he desired her on no account to give up mental prayer, and thus frustrate the work of grace in her soul, for who could say what an instrument for good she might become in the hands of God to the souls of others, if obedient now to the

[1] See *Histoire de Ste. Thérèse.*

heavenly calling? He bade her put away the thought of delusion, and thank God for His abundant grace, casting herself with confidence on His infinite love. But he prescribed an all-important rule : she was each day to take for the subject of her devotion some one mystery of the Passion of the Lord, and to draw from it some practical resolve. He also told her *never to seek* any sensible joy or emotion in prayer, but rather to mortify self in this. Who can describe the peace and repose of mind brought to Teresa by these words.

It was soon after this, when reciting the ' Veni Creator Spiritus,' that the grace of ecstasy was first vouchsafed to her, and she became entranced, or, as she describes, ' carried out of herself.' She had an intuitive consciousness that ' Jesus was always by her side, a witness of all that she did.' She relates that ' she saw no form, no similitude, but that she heard within her soul a Voice making her sensible of the Divine presence.' In Him was *her life*, and most surely the key-note of Teresa's spiritual history may be found in the aspiration of the Apostle, that he might ' know Him, and the power of His resurrection, and the fellowship of His sufferings.' But there were those who then, as now, doubted the possibility of ' knowing God' in this life as it was given to Teresa to know Him. Her friends still regarded her as deluded by Satan. Padranos had quitted Avila, and her new confessor, Father Alvarez, a man of eminent piety and austere virtue, seems to have thought it desirable that she should be less alone, and that she should abstain from frequent communion, as her most enraptured hours were connected with the Holy Sacrament.

Distracted by contrary directions, distrustful of herself, Teresa lifted up her troubled soul to the Lord, praying Him to undertake for her, and to deliver her from the

E

snares of the Evil One, saying, 'O my Lord, although all rise up against me, all created things persecute me, demons torment me, desert not one who putteth her sole trust in Thee.'

Immediately it seemed as though a Voice whispered to her innermost heart, 'Fear not, my daughter, *it is I.* Be not afraid ; I will not leave thee.' In a moment, she tells us, she found herself strong and tranquil. She knew that Christ had spoken to her soul, and she felt emboldened to declare before all the world what He had done for her.

For two more years Teresa had to bear the rebukes and reproaches which fell upon her, for all Avila grew to regard her as one possessed. Her confessor, Alvarez, alone defended her ; but the arrival of a man revered throughout Spain put an end to these trials and perplexities.

This was Peter of Alcantara, perhaps one of the most contemplative and enlightened of the band of saintly men who strove in this century to carry out a reform within the Spanish Church, and to revive its ancient fervour.

His presence in Avila was hailed with delight, and Teresa found in him the support she needed. Clothed in the coarsest raiment, bare-headed and bare-footed, regardless of sun or rain, heat or cold, enfeebled by age and austerities, Peter of Alcantara, with slow and wearied step, entered the gate of Avila. To Teresa, he was as the messenger from the Most High, the appointed means of bringing before her mind the great task to which her life was henceforth to be devoted—the Reform of her Order. They quickly understood one another ; she told him all that had disturbed her, whilst his long experience in those gifts which are supernatural, and his deep mystical knowledge, enabled him to uphold and strengthen her faith. He bade her 'rest in the full assurance that it was the work of God.' His sympathy was shown in his humbly admitting to her that he himself had felt 'the contradiction of good people one of the hardest trials,' but it was one to which she must accustom herself. To this holy old man she described the symbolic vision, which has since been so often represented in Christian art—the Angelic Messenger piercing her heart with the dart of Divine love. He bade her not be perplexed by these visions, but to 'continue her prayer with confidence, *neither wishing nor asking* for extraordinary graces, but accepting them when they came as from the hand of the Lord.'

The visit of Peter of Alcantara stirred within her a vehement desire to bring others nearer to God, and this was intensified by a strange and terrible vision, which she afterwards regarded as 'one of the Lord's greatest mercies to her.'

In this vision the anguish of a lost soul, the inward fire of remorse and despair, the outer darkness—all for a moment seemed revealed to her ; 'the pains of hell gat hold upon her,' and, when she came to herself, she was filled with a profound sense of her unworthiness, of 'the poverty of her outer life,' and of the infinite compassion of the Lord in delivering her soul from death. It was a call to her to arise and win other souls to God.

But the nuns of the Monastery of the Incarnation could not understand Teresa. When she spoke to them of mental prayer and of a higher life she was to them as a visionary —an enthusiast carried away by wild notions, unsuited to the ideas and habits of the age. They were content to remain as they were ; they saw no necessity for change or reform, and her words seemed to fall unheeded to the ground. But from this seed, apparently so insignificant

E 2

and trodden under foot, there arose a widespread moral reform in the Church of Spain, and a fresh spring of spiritual life, known as Catholic Mysticism.

Teresa's conventual experience had opened her eyes to the fact that vocal prayer—that is to say, the recital of prayers however thoughtfully repeated—could not *satisfy* the soul. She felt that there should be greater freedom ; the little child must cast itself without restraint into the Father's arms, speaking to Him in its own untutored language.

Mental prayer was therefore early adopted by Teresa, and—though, as we have seen, often interrupted for long intervals—became the germ of the mystical theology of which she was destined to be so great an exponent.

She divided mental prayer into four distinct stages : the stage of *recollectedness*, the stage of *quietude*, the stage of *union*, and the stage of *ecstasy* or *rapture*.

To illustrate her meaning, she compares the renewed soul to a garden—'the planting of the Lord'—but the soil, being by nature ungrateful, requires much weeding and watering. The Divine Master has sown good seed and planted goodly fruit trees, and we, as fellow-labourers with Him, must weed this garden and 'water the soil carefully, that it may produce fragrant blossom and fruit, so that He may often come and visit the garden which He hath planted, and find delight therein.' She describes four ways of watering the soil of this garden, corresponding with each of the four stages of prayer.

The first is with water drawn with difficulty from a deep well. The second is with water raised by a wheel and distributed by pipes over the soil. Thirdly, it may be watered by a running stream or brook. And fourthly, by balmy showers.

The first mode is laborious, and requires great patience and strength. We must in no wise rest till the Water of Life which God gives springs up within us. This represents the prayer of *recollectedness*, which is the first step in mental devotion. It requires great earnestness, and an entire concentration of the thoughts, the soul meanwhile 'looking and waiting for the Lord.'

The beginner may have to wait long before he becomes conscious of the Divine Presence ; dryness and weariness will at times almost overpower him ; the weakness of the body will often weigh down the soul, but if he has the courage to persevere in mental prayer he will surely have his reward ; the dry and thirsty land will become as a watered garden by the influx of the Spirit, and deep within the soul will spring up a devout sense of God's immediate Presence, and he will say with the patriarch of old, 'Surely God is in this place, and I knew it not.'

Courage and perseverance were ever insisted upon by Teresa ; but she also says, 'Before thou prayest, prepare thyself.' This must be done by devout meditation on the life of our Lord. We must *hold ourselves* in His Presence ; continuing in prayer in spite of dryness, languor, or feeble faith. 'The kingdom of Heaven is taken by force.' Like Jacob wrestling with the angel we must wrestle in prayer, saying, 'I will not let Thee go until Thou bless me.'

The second stage is that of *quietude*—or *contemplation*, as it is sometimes called.

Once more Teresa bids all who would enter upon this second stage 'to turn again and again before prayer to the Source of all good—*meditation* on the Passion of our Lord, for the nearer we draw unto God, the deeper will be our humility.'

She likens this stage of *quietude* to the work of the

labourer, who, by means of a wheel and water-pipes,
is able to draw more water for his garden and distribute
it with far less fatigue, not having to work continuously,
but being able to rest from time to time.   The soul
does not now require the same effort to concentrate the
thoughts, but has a profound sense of the Divine Presence within and around.   To use her words, 'the soul
is now touching upon something which is supernatural.
All its powers are gathered up within itself, yet these
powers are neither suspended nor asleep ; but the *will*
alone acts, and without knowing how, the soul surrenders
itself, and is led captive by the love of God.'   It is like the
holy repose of Mary at Bethany, sitting calm and still and
reverent at the feet of Jesus, looking upon Him and hearing
His word.

It is *listening* rather than speaking ; 'I will hearken to
what the Lord God will say unto me,' desiring only to be
drawn more and more out of self into union with Him.
'This state of blessed repose is not of long duration.   Like
St. Peter on the Mount of Transfiguration, the soul would
make here a tabernacle, but it is soon disturbed, and has
to descend from the Mount.   Indeed, any efforts in our
own strength to prolong this state of quietude would be like
laying logs of wood on a little spark—the spark would be
extinguished.   Let us simply understand that all we have
to do at those seasons when the soul is raised to this stage
of prayer is to be quiet and humble, laying on a few straws
—little acts of humility or words of love, and self-abandon-
ment, nothing more—and the spark of Divine love enkindled within the heart will become a great fire.'

The third stage is that of *union*.   Of this Teresa herself
says that she can tell us but little, as she could never
explain nor understand it ; but, she adds, 'the higher any-

onc has ascended, the greater reason has he to fear and lose all *self*-confidence.'

She compares this prayer of union to 'a running stream from a brook or river by which the garden is abundantly watered, the labourer having only to turn the stream into the proper channels. But now he is amazed to behold the Divine Master taking upon Himself the whole labour : " I, the Lord, do water it." He it is who now directs the stream, so that the labourer has but to rest and enjoy the celestial flowers which are beginning to appear and to put forth their fragrance.' In this prayer the soul receives a fresh baptism of the Spirit ; it is renewed in strength and deepened in humility ; it enters into a state of profound calm, 'resting in the Lord.' This is described by Teresa as a blissful sleep. ' I sleep, but my heart waketh—a sleep full of sweetness and delight, infinitely greater than in the former stages of prayer. The soul seems to die to all earthly things and to be athirst only for God, yea, even for the living God . . . like as the hart panteth after the water brooks, so longeth the soul after God.' The faculties of the mind are still ; the mysteries of Divine grace cannot be fathomed. The soul has entered into the secret place of the Most High ; it is abiding under the shadow of the Almighty, and its language is, 'Whom have I in heaven but Thee, and there is none upon earth to be desired besides Thee.'

The fourth stage is *ecstasy* or *rapture.*

Teresa likens this to a gracious rain which cometh down from heaven and refresheth the earth. It fills and saturates in its abundance the whole soil of the garden. It usually comes unexpectedly ; the labourer is taken by surprise, and sees the once dry land converted as by a miracle into a blooming paradise.

At these seasons, she says, 'the Divine Spirit floods the
soul with grace ; it hath a desire to enter within the courts
of the Lord—a longing that mortality may be swallowed
up of life. Even as a flame mounts upwards, so, inflamed
with Divine ardour, the soul seems to ascend above itself,
and before the thoughts can be collected, by a power which
is felt to be irresistible, it falls into a state of trance, as
though passing away, as though caught up in a cloud.
The first sensation is that of fear : the flesh and the heart
fail. Even as at the Transfiguration, the disciples feared
as they entered into the cloud, so the soul on the verge
of ecstasy is affrighted. But God is the strength of the
heart. It hears the voice saying, Fear not, it is I. An
absolute surrender of the whole being is made to Him, and
the soul wings its flight into the unseen, where fear is lost in
fruition.'

This state cometh 'not of him that willeth, nor of him
that runneth, but of God who giveth the increase.'

Teresa's life until 1561 was especially marked by the
frequency of her visions. In that year began a new phase
of her existence—the life of action—when she commenced
her great work of reform, a labour of love which she pursued with untiring energy for twenty years in spite of
poverty, ill-health, calumny, and persecution.

The disorder and immorality which prevailed, especially
in religious houses, disgraced the Church ; and to renovate
the whole Church through the reformation of the monastic
orders—to kindle the dying embers of spiritual devotion by
drawing men and women into closer communion with the
Lord and with the unseen world—this was the holy mission
undertaken by Teresa of Avila.

July 16 was a high day at the Convent of the Incarnation ; it was the great Festival of the Carmelites, and was observed with much pomp and ceremony. The chapel had been thronged throughout the day, and it was only as the shadows of evening were closing round that the crowd gradually dispersed. After the excitement of the Festival, Teresa would gladly have found herself alone, but she had no sooner retired to her cell than a group gathered there eager to converse with her. Among the number was her old friend Juana de Suarez and two nuns who had but lately taken the veil. With them came two girls, whose rich attire contrasted strangely with the sombre habit of the rest. These were Maria de Ocampo and her sister, cousins of Teresa. They had been educated in the monastery, and although now seemingly separated from Teresa by the divergence of their pursuits and tastes, they continued to be deeply attached to her, whilst she with disquietude watched the inroads which the world and its vanities had already made on their youthful hearts. The conversation turned on the events of the day, on the crowds of people present at the offices. Gradually they began to speak of the various hindrances to the religious life, the difficulty of maintaining a spirit of recollectedness whilst living in so large a community as that of the Incarnation, encompassed and disturbed as it was by so many visitors.

Maria de Ocampo listened eagerly to the conversation. Suddenly she broke in, exclaiming, 'Why should not we who are gathered here clear away these hindrances, and begin elsewhere another kind of life like that of the hermits of old? If indeed you possess the courage to follow in the track of the bare-footed Franciscans, why not found a new convent?' Teresa could hardly repress her astonishment. Could this indeed be Maria de Ocampo, hitherto absorbed by worldly pleasures, who spoke thus, and who was

the first openly to suggest to them all a higher life? To prove
the sincerity of her words, Maria at once offered a thousand
ducats of her own inheritance towards the foundation of
this new convent, where only a few nuns should be admitted.
All were delighted with the project. Teresa, tremulous
with joy, foresaw her long-cherished desire fulfilled, and
before they parted for the night plans were made, and a reformed convent already arose in their imagination. Funds
were immediately collected. The Primitive Carmelite rule
—long fallen into disuse—was to be restored, and a life of
prayer, poverty, and self-sacrifice, which Teresa held to be
the true imitation of Christ, was to be inaugurated in the
new convent.

To gather together a few who would lead such a life, she
regarded as the surest means of raising her order from its
low estate, and causing it again to shine forth as a light in
the surrounding darkness. The Provincial of the Carmelites
was consulted and gave the attempt his approval, promising
to acknowledge the new convent. Peter of Alcantara, whose
work of reform among the Franciscans had first suggested
the thought to Teresa, sanctioned it on all points, and
shortly afterwards, 'with the help of many prayers,' a house
was purchased, the necessary funds being unexpectedly provided by Teresa's eldest brother Lorenzo, who had been
for the last twenty years in Peru. He had had no commu-
nication from his sister, and had no knowledge whatever
consequently of her design; but it had suddenly come into
his mind to send her a certain sum of money as a present,
and this reached her precisely in time to defray the expense
incurred in the purchase and necessary arrangements of the
house.

Teresa did not fail to see the hand of God in this un-
looked-for help in a moment of extreme difficulty.

The love of Teresa for her family had never slackened ; her natural tenderness of heart had been intensified by her religion, so that it has been said, 'it seemed as though her human affections, passing through the heart of Jesus, had drawn forth a double vitality.' It was therefore an intense delight to her to be aided thus by her brother in the foundation of her little monastery.

But when the project of a new foundation got rumoured abroad, it caused such excitement and opposition that the Provincial withdrew his consent, and for some months the work was stayed.

Teresa's patience was sorely tried. Not only was the outer world adverse to her scheme, but the nuns of her community were deeply offended by what they considered presumption on her part.

The Monastery of the Incarnation dated from about the time of Teresa's birth. The nuns therefore had known no other rule but that which was called the ' *mitigated*,' a milder rule which had been conceded to the Carmelite Order in the preceding century by Pope Eugenius IV. To return now to the hard lines of the primitive rule, as Teresa proposed, was met by a storm of indignation.

Their present convent was commodious and filled with all the comforts of the time. ·The nuns were allowed full liberty and enjoyment ; they were not·bound by the stringent fasts and abstinences enjoined in former years, and they now resolutely set themselves against any change. ' Reform was a condemnation of the laxity which existed ; and this was resented by the lukewarm, whilst to the rest it appeared like temerity.'

Teresa meekly bent her head to the storm. ' To one who walks with eyes fixed on eternity the adversities of time give but little disquiet.' There was one characteristic especially remarkable in Teresa—this was her *good sense*, which never failed her. She possessed an extraordinary amount of tact and power of persuasion, and these are exhibited in every instance where she met with opposition. She accustomed herself never to complain of those who rose up against her, but on the contrary made excuses for them; and thus she softened the hearts of her opponents, and in the end generally won them over to her cause. Teresa's friends did not desert her in this emergency, and it was determined to apply to the Holy See and obtain, if possible, a Brief in favour of the new convent.

In the meanwhile the building was continued and the little chapel nearly finished, when a sudden order arrived which removed Teresa from Avila. Though looked upon with suspicion and even contumely at this time by many in her native city, the holy life of Teresa, and the extraordinary gifts bestowed upon her, had become known in other parts of Spain. Francis Borgia and Peter of Alcantara had borne witness to her fervent devotion, and to the intense reality of her faith.

Teresa's fame had reached the ears of Dona Luisa, Duchess de la Cerda, a young widow, overwhelmed with grief at the early death of her husband. Insensible alike to the caresses of her child and the devotion of her brother, her one desire in the midst of her desolation was that Teresa of Avila might be summoned to console her. In December 1561 an order was accordingly obtained from the Provincial of the Carmelites, in obedience to which Teresa started at once for Toledo. There a great change awaited her. She who longed for a life of poverty and simplicity found herself lodged in a palace, surrounded by a princely retinue, and treated with the utmost homage by all. She was received as an angel of consolation, sent to bring healing to the sorrow-stricken widow. For six months Teresa remained at Toledo, and before she left, her persuasive eloquence and tender sympathy had the effect of arousing the conscience as well as soothing the sorrow of Luisa de la Cerda, who arose from the state of depression in which Teresa had found her, resolved to devote the remainder of her life to the service of God.

 Whilst at Toledo, Teresa, by order of her spiritual director,[1] wrote the history of her inner life—a task most uncongenial to one who would gladly have put aside all thought of self ; but, in obedience to him, she was forced to retrace her past life, step by step, analysing all her acts, and giving a faithful record of the whole course of her experience.

In June 1562, Teresa received permission from the Provincial of the Carmelites to return to Avila ; and, the very night of her arrival, the long-expected Brief was received from Rome. By this Brief, Pope Pius IV.[2] sanctioned the establishment of the new monastery of St. Joseph under primitive Carmelite rule. But it was to be subject to the Bishop of Avila, *not* to the Provincial of the Carmelites. Teresa being a nun of the Incarnation, her name did not appear ; she was still in subjection to the Superior of that house. Some fresh difficulties arose as to revenue, but, fortunately for Teresa, Peter of Alcantara was at this critical moment in Avila, and it was 'the approbation of this holy old man,' Teresa says, 'and the great trouble he took, which did the whole work ; ' for, through his good offices, the Bishop was won over to accept the new foundation without revenue. ' It seemed,' she adds, 'as though Peter of Alcantara's life had been preserved till this affair was ended ; for he had been ill for more than two years, and died almost immediately after.'

---

[1] Father Ibañez. [2] Cardinal de Medici.

It was privately decided that there should be no further
delay in opening the monastery, and on August 24, 1562—
being the Festival of St. Bartholomew—mass was celebrated
for the first time in the little chapel by direction of the
Bishop, Teresa being present. Four dowerless orphans
were arrayed in the religious habits which she had provided for them, and these four composed the community.
The dress consisted of a coif and veil of coarse white
linen, and a white woollen cloak over a petticoat of the
natural colour of the wool.

The 'Te Deum Laudamus' was chanted by those who
assisted at the simple ceremony, and the little bell of St.
Joseph's rang out vigorously, revealing to the inhabitants of
Avila the secret of the inauguration, and announcing to the
astonished nuns of the Incarnation the unwelcome birth of
the new monastery. The consternation and excitement
were intense. A crowd gathered in the streets of Avila,
threatening to pull down the new building, and ready to
stone the foundress.

A messenger was immediately despatched to St. Joseph's
by the Prioress of the Incarnation, requiring Teresa at
once to return to her own convent. She maintained her
outward calmness, but doubt and discouragement took
hold upon her. As a nun of the Incarnation, she was
bound to obey the order of the Prioress, but she dreaded
being detained at the monastery, and for ever separated
from her newly formed convent. She was fully aware
that she had incurred the anger of both the Provincial
and the Prioress—the inauguration having been accomplished without their knowledge and consent—and her
spirit became full of heaviness and forebodings of evil.
But in this dark hour her watchword came home with
power—

Let nothing disturb thee.
Let nothing alarm thee.
All things pass away.
God is unchangeable.

She obeyed the summons of the Prioress, and passed on foot through the town of Avila, unmoved by the tumult and threatening looks of the people collected in the streets.

On arriving at the Convent of the Incarnation she was led as a culprit into the presence of the Prioress, who was surrounded by her nuns. The Provincial of the Carmelites was to pass judgment upon her. He reprimanded her severely ; she abstained from all attempt at self-justification, but knelt down and humbly asked his forgiveness. The Provincial was touched by her humility, and, remembering that he had himself at first encouraged her in the foundation of the new monastery, he was the more disposed towards indulgence. But the exasperated nuns renewed their charges, saying 'that she was setting up novelties, and causing scandal in the city.'

Still Teresa was silent, until ordered by the Provincial to declare openly before the whole community her motives for the course she had taken. Simply and calmly she narrated what had passed, and how she had been led to found the new monastery. Impressed by her words, neither the Provincial nor those present found just reason for condemnation.

The authorities of the city were not so easily appeased ; the Governor of Avila demanded that the new monastery should be closed and the novices dismissed. In spite of the Papal Brief and the consent of the Bishop, the city authorities refused to allow a religious house without revenue to be established in Avila. In the end, however, Teresa triumphed ; the Monastery of St. Joseph was not closed, and in Lent 1563 she received permission to return there, accompanied by four nuns of the Incarnation.

The tide of popular feeling turned ; those who had been her most vehement opponents became her warmest sup- porters, and from this period dates the beginning of that great work of religious reform which has made the name of Teresa venerated in Spain, and honoured throughout Chris- tendom.

For five happy years Teresa never quitted the Monastery of St. Joseph ; these were, she says, 'the most tranquil of her life, the calm and rest of which she often missed in after years.'

The number of nuns was limited to thirteen.[1] At the Incarnation there had been one hundred and eighty, and the largeness of the community had been regarded by Teresa as a great hindrance to advancement in the religious life. Her desire, therefore, was to draw together a few devout sisters who would give themselves to prayer, not merely for themselves, but for the Church of God, and who would pray especially for those wanderers who never prayed for themselves. The one great object which she proposed to her nuns was *constant intercessory prayer.* 'Help me, my sisters,' she said, 'in praying for others. It is for this end that you have been brought together by the Lord. This is your vocation. It may seem hard to some of you to pray for others rather than for yourselves, but what prayer is better in the sight of God than intercessory prayer?'

The new Carmelites being strictly cloistered had no external work ; it was the more necessary, therefore, that they should be few in number, so that within the cloister there should be sufficient employment to call forth all their energies. There were no lay sisters ; all the household

[1] It was afterwards raised to twenty.

work was therefore done by the nuns, Teresa herself taking her share of the labour. Wherever her work, she felt that ' *this* was her appointed place, and here she would meet the Lord as surely as in her cell.'

Teresa knew well how to make the life of recollectedness and prayer a life of pleasantness as well as of peace. They lived as one family, having all things in common, joys and sacrifices—ever ready to help each other in the daily life— by love serving one another. At the hour for recreation, Teresa encouraged great gaiety of heart, and gave the example. She was so persuaded that it was impossible to keep up at all times the same degree of restraint, and that if attempted it would have disastrous effects on both soul and body, that she regarded these seasons of recreation as most important, and expected each one of the community to do her best to enliven the others. ' Do not imitate,' she said, 'those persons who no sooner become somewhat devout than they assume a sour and severe look, as if afraid to talk lest their devotion should take wing.'

It was thus that Teresa led her sisters in the way of holy charity. She was strict with them, but gentle, simple and practical in all things. To win their confidence she would descend to their level, as though she were but a babe in spiritual attainments, her soul the meanwhile continually rejoicing in the full consciousness of the Lord's presence and of His Divine guidance.

She recalls in her description of the Lord's dealings with her those words spoken of Israel's lawgiver : 'The Lord spake unto him face to face, as a man speaketh unto his friend.' ' I know,' she says in her ' Vita,' ' that although He is the Lord, I can commune with Him as with *a friend*. He is not like the princes of this earth, who maintain their dignity by state and grandeur. He is God, yet is He man, and our weaknesses excite no surprise in Him who knows our nature, and that our frail flesh is liable to frequent falls. . . . We need no one to introduce us ceremoniously into His presence, for freely and without restraint does He let us approach Him.'

The little chapel of the new monastery was always filled, and among the crowd of women who gathered there day by day to attend the office none was more constant than Maria de Ocampo. She placed herself as close as possible to the grating which shut in the nuns, as though she would gain something by closer contact. She knelt there richly dressed and radiant in beauty, her eyes moist with tears, whilst she listened to the slow solemn chant of the Carmelites. It was, however, but a passing emotion, for no sooner had she left the chapel than the world drew her back within its alluring net.

But in a few months the prayer of Teresa and her nuns, which had been constantly offered up for her, was fully answered. Maria came, and, throwing herself at Teresa's feet, asked for the coarse cloth dress of a Carmelite. She was received as a novice. All her jewels and her fortune were offered to the convent, but Teresa would not accept the proffered wealth. 'She would take no gain of money.' Poverty was the rule of the house, and it was a treasure she would not part with.

It was at this time that Teresa was directed by her confessor to continue the record of her life which she had begun whilst at Toledo. He also required her to write out a summary of her daily instructions to the nuns, and thus it was that the 'Way of Perfection' was produced.[1]

It was about the end of the year 1566 that a new object

---

[1] Her other works are the *Book of the Foundations, The Interior Castle,* an Exposition of the Canticles (the greater part of which, how-

was presented to Teresa's religious energy. A Franciscan monk of the name of Maldonado, a missionary but lately returned from the Spanish Indies, arrived at St. Joseph's and asked for an interview with the Prioress.

Teresa was greatly moved by his account of the misery and ignorance he had witnessed in these distant Spanish possessions, where the name of Christ was almost unknown and the unhappy natives treated with the greatest cruelty. The compassion and enthusiasm of Teresa were excited to the highest pitch. Her mind was filled with the thought of these 'dark places of the earth, full of habitations of cruelty,'[1] and she resolved to aid to the utmost of her power in dispelling the darkness by sending to the oppressed natives the blessed light of the Gospel.

To her there appeared no other way of effecting this object except through the establishment of friars of the Reformed Carmelite rule—men who should be trained to mission work, full of burning zeal and devotion, who would gladly peril their lives to bring these poor heathen souls into Christ's fold.

Teresa and her nuns ceased not to pray that a way might be opened for carrying out this design, but six months passed without any result. In the following spring (1567) Teresa was somewhat disturbed by learning that the General of the Carmelites, who always resided in Rome, was expected shortly at Avila. She felt that he might be displeased at the withdrawal of her new convent from his jurisdiction ; she herself, by her early vows, was still subject to his authority, and she dreaded lest he should order her back to the Monastery of the Incarnation. To remove all prejudice from his mind was her first object, and to this

ever, was burnt by her confessor), her *Constitution*, and *Exclamations of the Soul to God.*   [1] Psalm lxxiv. 20.

F

end, having obtained the permission of her Bishop, she
adopted the well-conceived plan of inviting him at once to
honour her convent with a visit.   Accordingly, Fra Giovanni
Battista Rubeo—the Father-General of the Carmelites—on
reaching Avila came immediately to St. Joseph's.   She narrated
to him all the circumstances of the foundation, and, far from
blaming her, he, to her great joy, approved of all that she
had done, and only regretted that, through the vacillation
of the Provincial, the convent had been placed under the
Bishop of the diocese.

Fra Rubeo proved to be as desirous of reform in the
Carmelite order as Teresa herself, and great was his satisfaction to find in Avila one who had successfully commenced
the work which he had so much at heart.   Through Teresa's
instrumentality Father Rubeo now looked for a widespread
revival of spirituality throughout Spain, and she received
from him the command not only to found other convents
for women, but also to form two monasteries in Castile for
men of the Reformed rule.   Before returning to Rome an
arrangement was also made with the Bishop of Avila, by
which the Monastery of St. Joseph was again placed under
the jurisdiction of the General of the Carmelites.

Teresa was now fifty-two years old, but 'the spark of
that first deathless fire yet buoyed her up,' and without
hesitation she bade farewell to her peaceful home and life
of seclusion at St. Joseph's, to sally forth again into the
outer world, to encumber herself with business, and devote
all her energies to the newly appointed task.

She met with no encouragement from her friends ; the
same difficulties which she had encountered in the foundation of the Monastery of St. Joseph, had again to be overcome, but she made light of all these troubles, and before
long a new convent for women was founded at Medina del

Campo. Her mind, however, was especially occupied with the thought of that other work confided to her—the foundation of two monasteries for men. An unexpected friend was raised up at Medina in the Prior of the Carmelites of the Mitigated rule—Fra Antonio de Heredia. She spoke to him in private of her design, and learnt that he himself had felt called to a life of higher devotion, and earnestly begged to be received as her first Reformed friar.

Heredia was no longer young, and Teresa hesitated ; but finally consented, insisting, however, on his submitting to a year's probation.

A few days afterwards she met with the man whose name was to be ever associated with hers in the work of reform—this was Juan de la Cruz, the most mystical of Spanish Mystics, and whom she at once accepted as the first friar of the new Order.

In 1568 the first monastery for friars of the Primitive Carmelite rule was formed at Durvelo, and as no work of Teresa's reflects greater honour upon her name, so none brought upon her greater trials. Monastery after monastery arose for women. Her utter want of means to carry out her work excited continual remonstrance from her friends but the question of money never weighed upon Teresa. She had implicit trust that God would supply all her need. When at Toledo she possessed but three ducats wherewith to begin the new convent. In vain her friends expostulated. She cheerfully replied, ' Teresa and three ducats are indeed *nothing* ; but *God*, Teresa, and three ducats can accomplish it.'

A second Reformed Monastery for men was formed at Pastrana. The house was presented to her by Ruy Gomez, Prince of Eboli, who was high in favour at the Court of Philip II. On the arrival of Teresa at Pastrana, she was received with every mark of deference by Ruy Gomez. The Princess of Eboli was desirous of founding also a convent for Reformed Carmelite nuns ; both these houses were established at Pastrana.   But in the midst of success there were not wanting elements of trouble.   Difficulties arose with the Princess of Eboli.   She had by some means become aware that Teresa had written a private account of her own spiritual life, and nothing would satisfy the Princess but to read it.   Her curiosity would not be restrained. For a long time Teresa resisted her importunity, and only at length reluctantly yielded at the request of the Prince, and on the condition that what she had written *should be shown to no one else.*   But the Princess was as indiscreet as she was wilful.   The book was read by everyone in the palace, where it excited much gossip and criticism, and was ultimately brought under the notice and suspicion of the Inquisition.   The labour which Teresa underwent in founding religious houses was cheerfully, even joyfully borne. She made light of all privations, though often suffering from ill-health.   But her most difficult task, she says, was to adapt herself to the various tempers with which she came in contact.   The Princess of Eboli was one of those who tried her patience to the utmost ; but Teresa possessed an intuitive insight into character, and her extraordinary gift of tact, joined to her gentleness and large-heartedness, seldom failed to win over those who were at first most troublesome and contradictory.

New monasteries arose at Salamanca and Alva de Tormes ; the last-named, after a few more years of toil, became her burial-place, where to this day Spanish devotees kneel before her shrine.

About this time Pope Pius V. appointed two new visitors to inspect the Carmelite monasteries in Spain.   In Anda-

lusia great disorder prevailed among the Mitigated friars.
The visitation of Father Rubeo—the General of the Carmelites—seven years previous to this, had been without effect.
The unruly friars withstood all reformatory regulations.
On the present occasion two Dominicans were chosen.
Father Vargas was sent to Andalusia, and Father Hernandez to Castile. The latter was a man of much pru-
dence as well as piety. Reforms were instituted with great
judgment. His authority extended over the whole order in
Castile—Mitigated and Primitive—and so impressed was he
by the sanctity of those houses under Teresa's rule, that he
recommended a further extension of these establishments—
the number for men having been hitherto limited to *two* by
Father Rubeo, *and those two in Castile.* He also appointed
Teresa Prioress of the Incarnation, with the hope that a
reform might be effected in that monastery through her
wise intervention.

Nothing could have been more uncongenial to Teresa
than this appointment, or less welcome to the nuns over
whom she was to rule, for they stoutly maintained their old
opposition to any ' novelties.'

She remained at the Incarnation for three years, during
which time she never sought to impose upon the nuns the
austerities of the Primitive rule which she herself followed,
but to which they were not bound, but simply sought to in-
fuse the spirit of love into their observance of the Mitigated
rule. After a while her gentle words, and the commanding
influence of a holy life, bore fruit ; gradually and imper-
ceptibly the nuns turned from worldly things, and dedicated
themselves anew to the service of God.

A great change had taken place in Teresa since she was
herself a nun in the Monastery of the Incarnation. Her
spiritual life was no longer marked by the visions and

ecstasies of former years. Such manifestations were not
needed now, and they had become rare. Profound peace
reigned within the soul *possessed* by Christ; the life of self
was dead, and she could say with the Apostle, 'Mihi enim
vivere Christus est.' No longer absorbed in contemplation, it seemed as though she had been recalled to earth,
endued with more than human ardour to work for God, and
to bring others to labour in His vineyard with the same
deep living sense of His Presence.

At Veas, where she had gone to found a new monastery
for nuns, she met for the first time Jerome Gratian, whose
life was destined to be closely interwoven with hers in the
trials and difficulties which beset her latter years.

Gratian had been for three years a friar of her order.
He had won the hearts of his brethren at Pastrana by his
piety and humility; added to this he had great eloquence
and a remarkable talent for administration. The Discalced
friars had been introduced into Andalusia by Father Vargas,
the apostolic visitor for that province, and the intelligence
and address of Gratian had so won his esteem, that in spite
of Gratian's opposition, Vargas unwisely determined to
make him his deputy in the important office of visitor to
the Carmelite monasteries throughout Andalusia; an act of
imprudence which raised grave disputes between the Mitigated and Discalced friars, and imperilled the reform instituted by Teresa. Gratian was but thirty years old, and
grievous offence was given by the elevation of so young and
inexperienced a man to so important a post.

In spite of all the tact and consideration displayed by
Gratian, the Mitigated friars took alarm and wrote to Rome
to the General of the Carmelites, acquainting him with the
undue partiality shown by Vargas to the Discalced friars, and
assuring him that their rule was menaced by the appointment

of Gratian to the office of visitor. Father Rubeo's wrath was kindled. His desire for reform throughout the order was sincere, but he did not desire that it should be effected by *forcing* the rule of the Discalced friars on those of the Mitigated rule. He now looked with suspicion on a movement which bordered on schism, and which bid fair to endanger the peace and prosperity of the whole order.

He therefore obtained a brief from Pope Gregory XIII. revoking the powers bestowed on the two apostolic visitors; but Ormaneto, the Pope's Nuncio in Spain, was equally determined to retain them. He reinstated Vargas as visitor in Andalusia, and appointed Gratian as his coadjutor, writing at the same time to the Papal See a full account of all the circumstances. The result was that Ormaneto, being on the spot, was given full liberty to act as he deemed best.

Teresa's foundations had hitherto been confined to Castile, by order of Rubeo; but at this critical time she was urged by Gratian to found a new monastery at Seville and in an evil hour obeyed. It was to her the commencement of the way of sorrows. It at once brought upon her the charge of disobedience from Father Rubeo.

In May 1575 she set out for Seville, accompanied by six of her nuns. Cordova, the ancient capital of Moorish Spain, 'the Gem of the South,' was reached on Whitsun eve. At an early hour the following morning, that they might be seen by no one, Teresa and her nuns made their way over the old bridge which still crosses the Guadalquivir, and, passing through the narrow streets, reached the church to which they had been directed as the most retired in Cordova. But, being a day of Festival, they found to their dismay an immense crowd already assembled outside. At the approach of Teresa and her nuns, clad in their white woollen cloaks, with veiled faces and sandalled feet, the crowd

became greatly excited, so much so that Teresa tells us that
'these were some of the worst moments she ever experienced, for there was such a tumult at their appearance,
that it was as though an entry of *bulls* had taken place for
the national sport.'

Seville was reached towards the end of May, when earth
and sky were bright with the glory of a southern spring.
Teresa and her little company alighted at a small hired
house in the Calle de las Armas, where the harassing fact
was made known to her that no permission had been accorded by the Archbishop of Seville for the foundation of
the new monastery ; and that, moreover, he had instituted a
rule by which no religious establishment could be admitted
within Seville without sufficient funds to make it self-sup
porting.   A month passed without the required licence, but
at length a letter from Gratian induced the Archbishop to
visit Teresa, and the cause of the Carmelites was won.   As
it had been with others, so was it with the Archbishop, he
could not resist the spell of Teresa's influence.   He left her,
bidding her 'do what she liked, and as she liked, for the
glory of God.'   That very day the house was consecrated as
a cloistered building.

It was a close and incommodious dwelling, and the
whole community, unaccustomed to the heat of southern
Spain, suffered much from the overcrowding ; but fortunately at this juncture Teresa's brother, Lorenzo de Cepeda,
arrived from the Indies with his family.   He had given
Teresa unexpected aid some years previously, and he now
again came forward to help her.   A suitable house was purchased by him at once, to which he added a chapel.

In May 1576 the convent was ready for occupation.
Teresa would have taken possession quietly, but the Archbishop determined otherwise.   The streets of Seville were

gaily decorated, and a procession formed by all the clergy and confraternities of the city, whilst the Archbishop himself carried the Holy Sacrament. At the threshold of the convent Teresa knelt to receive his benediction ; but he, in the presence of all, bent down and asked her to bless him.

Teresa, about this time, had the satisfaction of learning that the record of her life, which had so long been under the scrutiny of the Inquisition, had at length received a favourable verdict. But this triumph was followed by a far more severe ordeal. Her orthodoxy was again brought in question, and false reports were circulated as to the observances of the new convent. A foolish novice, who had been dismissed, accused Teresa of ' confessing the nuns,' and this charge, taken up by a credulous priest, was made the ground for again denouncing her to the Inquisition.

Unusual publicity was given to the proceedings against her. The whole city was in a stir. The gates of the convent were closely guarded, no egress was permitted. The crowded streets, through which the Inquisitors had to pass on their way to the convent, were lined with horsemen— emissaries of the Holy Office. Through all the turmoil Teresa remained calm and serene. She was minutely questioned, but her answers were clear and satisfactory.

The Inquisitors declared that she had been unjustly accused, and the carriages which had been brought to convey Teresa and the nuns away as prisoners, returned empty. But the matter did not rest here. The Inquisitors wished to investigate further Teresa's method of prayer, and her instructions to her nuns. She therefore drew up two documents, in which she gave a full account of the different stages of prayer through which she herself had passed, and also the simple method of devotion which she had adopted for her nuns. The Inquisitors expressed themselves satisfied,

and not only ceased from all further proceedings against
Teresa, but publicly censured the priest who had denounced
her. From henceforth there was peace with the Holy Office ;
but another struggle, longer and more painful, was before her.

All this time the conflict had been going on with increasing violence between the Mitigated and Reformed friars.
A general Chapter had been held by Father Rubeo at Pia-
cenza, where severe decrees were fulminated against 'those
rebels who, under the name of Discalced Carmelites, had
founded monasteries without the consent of the General of
the Order.' A Portuguese friar, of the name of Tostado,
was also despatched to Spain, with full power to put an end
to 'the anarchy which prevailed among the Carmelites,
through the revolt of these innovators.' The Discalced friars
were to be driven out of their monasteries, whilst serious accusations were brought against Teresa herself. She was for-
bidden to make any further foundations, and was ordered to
retire into one of her monasteries, and not to leave it, on any
pretext whatever. This was, in other words, imprisonment.

Teresa submitted without remonstrance. She had a
peace within which nothing could disturb—'a communion
with God, rich and deep, drowning every sorrow and provo-
cation in its calm, mighty depths.'

Toledo was fixed upon as her place of detention. She
had long foreseen that there was but one way by which
peace could be secured to the Carmelite Order. This was
by the formation of a separate province for the Reformed
friars. To attempt any amalgamation whilst the feeling of
hostility was so strong would be utterly futile. Ormaneto
(the Pope's Nuncio) was entirely in favour of this arrangement ; all the necessary regulations were on the point of
being settled ; peace seemed about to be attained, when
the Nuncio died (1577).

His successor, Monsignor Sega, took a totally different view of the case. He determined at once to suppress all the Reformed monasteries. He regarded Teresa as a restless busybody, intractable and contumacious, as well as a despiser of the Apostolic precept, which permits not women to teach. His first act was to require Gratian to resign the office of visitor bestowed upon him by Ormaneto, and this not being complied with, harsher measures followed. All the leaders of the Reform movement had to fly from Andalusia, and Teresa, by direction of Gratian, was removed from Toledo to Avila. She was again in her native city, in her beloved Monastery of St. Joseph, but no longer free. Antonio de Heredia and Jerome Gratian were seized and imprisoned by order of Sega. In the midst of this persecution the office of Prioress of the Incarnation became vacant, and, to the indignation of Tostada, the nuns immediately elected Teresa. He insisted on another election, but the nuns persisted in voting for their old Prioress. As each separate suffrage was brought to the Provincial, he angrily tore it up and burnt it before the eyes of the offending nun, pronouncing her to be 'excommunicate and accursed.' It required Teresa herself to intervene before they would accept another Prioress *even as Teresa's deputy.* In revenge, Tostada seized and imprisoned Juan de la Cruz, the confessor of the nuns. Everywhere the Discalced friars were oppressed ; all seemed over with the Reform ; but, when others were cast down and dismayed, 'the spirit of Teresa alone enjoyed serenity and confidence.' 'We must suffer troubles,' were her words, 'but this Order will not perish.'

The end of the struggle was in truth approaching though the recall of Tostado to Rome and the death of Father Rubeo in 1578 had brought no respite.

Several prelates now interfered, and represented to Monsignor Sega that his severity was excessive. Among those who took up the cause of reform was Hernandez—the former apostolic visitor in Castile—and the Nuncio was startled to find that he himself was censured by so many men of high repute for the course he had pursued.

After a careful review of all that had taken place, he was led to admit the mistakes into which he had fallen. The decree by which the Reformed monasteries had been abolished was rescinded, Gratian was restored to his office, Juan de la Cruz and Heredia set free, and Teresa released from her detention at St. Joseph's. Finally, in 1580, a Brief was obtained from the Pope (Gregory XIII.) by which the Discalced were separated from the Mitigated Carmelites. Their monasteries were thenceforth formed into separate provinces, governed by a provincial of their own rule, and by this means peace was at length restored to the whole Order.

Old age with its infirmities had sapped the strength of Teresa, and she had had a stroke of paralysis in 1580, yet she continued to obey the calls made upon her for new foundations.

She lived to see founded fifteen houses of Reformed friars and seventeen of nuns, her friars being sent forth as missionaries to all parts of the world, preaching the Gospel to the ignorant and oppressed.

The end was near at hand. She spent the first day of the year 1582 at Avila, at her first Reformed Monastery of St. Joseph ; the following day she left it never to return. No relaxation was hers in this life. Feeble in body but strong in will, she started, regardless of the intense cold, for Burgos, there to found a new monastery for nuns. Whilst in that city she was in great danger from an inundation of the river Arlanzon, on the banks of which the new convent was built. The continual rains had caused the river to over-flow, and the turbid sluggish stream suddenly became a rushing mighty torrent. Trees were uprooted, and fell with a fearful crash ; houses tottered, whilst, like a surging sea, the swollen river held on its course, bearing along with it the wreckage it had made.

The inhabitants hastened up to the heights above the city, crying to the Carmelites to follow them. But it was too late. Teresa and her nuns took refuge in the highest chamber of the convent, whither they had carried the Holy Sacrament, and passed the anxious hours in prayer, without food, and in momentary expectation that the house would fall. In the night the waters abated, and an attempt was made by the people of Burgos to save the nuns. Certain men of the city swam to the convent, and breaking the doors made a way for the pent waters to flow out, and the Carmelites were rescued from the peril which threatened them. The calmness and intrepidity shown by Teresa during the inundation became quickly noised abroad, and she received a perfect ovation wherever she appeared. But she shrank from notice ; praise had become distasteful to the aged saint, and she rebuked with severity those who ventured to tell her that the rapid subsidence of the flood was regarded by the populace as a miracle wrought by her presence. From flattering words and marks of deference she would turn away, and say in low tones, 'Spare me, I pray you.' Her humility increased with her years, and by degrees she was given such a profound contempt for the honour which cometh from man, that she ceased to observe when at any time it was lacking.

She was never free now from suffering, and though partially paralysed, made light of all her ailments. It was her maxim that '*the less attention paid to these things the better one found oneself.*' Her tenderness towards other sufferers was most touching to witness. She would drag herself to the infirmary in the night to soothe and calm by her words any who were in pain. 'The longer I live,' she wrote, 'the more clearly do I see that love must be the ruling principle. I do not govern now with the same severity as formerly. I know not whether it is that my nuns never give me occasion to exercise it, or whether experience has proved to me *that the way of love is the best.*'

The slightest service, the least token of interest or affection, drew forth her gratitude, and she never failed to remember in her prayers those who had shown her kindness, ever asking God to reward them tenfold.

But the special trait in her character was her forbearance towards those who had injured her.

' To enjoy to the full the good graces of Mother Teresa,' said one of the Cardinals, 'one must have spoken ill of her, or caused her pain.'

She quitted Burgos at the end of July 1582, glad to escape from the veneration of which she had been the object, and to retire to the seclusion of St. Joseph's Monastery, where her young niece, Teresita—whom she had educated—was to make her profession. By order of the Father Provincial, however, she was obliged first to inspect the convents established at Palencia, Valladolid, and Medina del Campo. Her increasing debility occasioned alarm to her nuns, and they watched with anxiety her faltering steps as she passed from her cell to the choir.

At Medina she was met by Fra Antonio de Heredia, one of her first two friars, who came with a message from the Duchess of Alva, urgently requesting her to visit Alva. She again yielded up her own wishes, and being placed in a litter was carried to Alba de Tormes. She endured great privations during the journey, which lasted five days—food being scarce in the villages through which they passed— and her weakness became so great, that at times she swooned away. A carriage was sent by the Duchess when she heard of Teresa's illness, but when, on the evening of September 20, they reached Alba de Tormes, she was so exhausted that it was found impossible to proceed further, the palace of the Duchess being at a considerable height above the town. She was therefore conveyed to the convent, where she was received with every mark of loyalty and love. To the surprise of all, she rose early the next morning, and attended mass. The power of her will was unabated, though weighed down by bodily infirmity, and she insisted upon going over the convent, expressing pleasure at the order which prevailed. For some days she appeared to rally, and exhibited the most extraordinary energy, accompanying the nuns each morning to chapel, reciting the office and communicating ; but on September 29—the Festival of St. Michael and All Angels—after assisting at mass, she became so faint and feeble, that she had to be carried from the chapel. She directed the nuns to place her in a room where through a grated window the choir could be seen, and the office heard. She remained calm and silent throughout the remainder of the day, laid on the bed from which she was never more to rise.

'Love's blessed race' was run—the desired haven was at hand, 'when she would pass out of exile,' and be for ever with her Lord.

Tears were on every face, grief in every heart but hers, for Heaven was opening to her gaze, and her eye was lit up with joyful expectation.

All through the night she was holding communion with

G

the unseen ; and it was only by a smile of thanks to those
who gave her the prescribed remedies that she seemed to
return to earth.   At break of day on October 2, after a
sleepless night spent in prayer, Teresa sent for Father
Antonio that he might hear her confession.   He implored
her to pray that she might yet be spared to them for some
years.   ' Be not troubled, my brother,' she replied, ' I am
no longer needed here.'

The next evening at sunset, on the Vigil of St. Francis
Teresa asked for the sacred Viaticum.   The nuns gathered
around her, waiting for the arrival of Father Antonio and
anxiously hoping for a word of farewell, or a last counsel
from those lips so soon to be silent.   Teresa's eyes were
closed and her hands clasped together in supplication ; her
lips moved in prayer, and the words of the ' Miserere ' were
faintly heard : ' *Cor contritum et humiliatum, Deus, non de-
spicies,*' ' *Cor mundum crea in me, Deus.*'

At length she gazed around her, and extended her hands
to the kneeling nuns, whilst with eyes moist with tears she
prayed them 'to forgive her the evil example she had but
too often given them, for she was a great sinner.'   She bade
them ' avoid her faults, and strive to follow out exactly and
entirely the rule and constitutions of their order.'   Sobs
were the only response.

The sound of the bell now announced that the priest
had come.   As soon as he entered her cell with the Holy
Sacrament, Teresa, in spite of her pain and extreme weakness, raised herself up without help, and knelt on her bed.
Her face became bright and radiant with joy, and out of the
abundance of her heart she burst forth in these words :
'O my beloved Lord and my Spouse, the desired hour so
long wished for is come ! the time is come for me to meet
Thee, to behold Thee, and to depart from this life.   Blessed

be this hour! Happy and prosperous may the journey prove. Thy will, O Lord, be done. The hour is at hand when I shall pass out of this exile and go forth to Thee, to be united to Thee, to enjoy that Presence for which I have so long panted.'

Often in lone night watches she had thought of the hour when she would hear His voice, saying, 'Rise up, and come away;' and now the glad summons had come. 'Behold, the Bridegroom cometh! go ye out to meet Him:' and she arose to receive the symbol of His love before departing hence, and beholding face to face Him Whom her soul loved. Deep joy was given her, but with it was ever blended the undertone of humiliation. 'A broken and contrite heart, O God, Thou wilt not despise.' These were words uttered again and again by the dying saint.

Often, too, she dwelt on her being 'a daughter of the Church.' 'I die a daughter of the Church;' but deeper still lay the glorious foundation of her faith. She brought no other plea for her acceptance than the redemption through the precious blood of Christ. All the good works of her life which had won the praise of men, all that by the grace of God she had *done*, seemed to have faded now from her memory. They were as shifting sand in that supreme hour. She built not upon these, but prayed those around her to ask God to pardon all her sins, for her hope of salvation rested solely on the merits of her Divine Lord.'[1]

As night set in, she asked for the Sacrament of extreme unction, and joined with the nuns in the Penitential Psalms and Litany. When the ceremony was concluded, Father Antonio asked her whether she desired that her body after death should be carried to Avila? This question seemed to grieve her. She only answered, 'Is it for me to decide?

[1] *Histoire de Sainte Thérèse*, tome ii. p. 429.

Will they not in charity give me here a little corner of earth?' Throughout that night the pains of death encompassed her, and she was heard softly whispering the name of Jesus. That Name was to her as ointment poured forth, and she called upon Him to soothe and help her in her extremity.

The prayer of her youthful days was also murmured forth, ' Domine, da mihi hanc aquam.' Soon she would reach the river's brink, and take of the Water of Life freely. When at daybreak, on October 4, clean white linen sleeves and a fresh coif were brought her, she smiled sweetly; it seemed like arraying her for the marriage supper of the Lamb to which she was called; and she tenderly embraced the sister, laying her head on her shoulder, as if to thank her.

As the day wore on she seemed absorbed in contemplation; her head was supported by the sister who for thirteen years had been her constant companion. In her hand she held a crucifix, grasping it firmly to the end.

No words were uttered to those around her, but she appeared to be listening to a Voice inaudible to all but herself, to which she was responding. At times there was a look of wonder on her face, and then one of ineffable delight as she drew near to the eternal shore.

Reverently the priest and nuns knelt around her bed; hushed was every sound. That poor cell was to them transformed into the gate of Heaven,[1] for to those sad watchers it seemed as though

> the place was bright
> With something of Celestial light.[2]

So calm and peaceful was the end, that only a gentle

---

[1] See *Histoire de Sainte Thérèse*, tome ii. p. 431.
[2] See *Christian Year* (Visitation and Communion of the Sick).

sigh revealed to them the moment when the immortal spirit entered into rest.

On Thursday, October 4, on the Festival of St. Francis, at nine o'clock in the evening, Teresa of Avila passed away from this earth. 'She came into this world in the spring-tide, at the first streak of dawn, March 1515, and the Lord called her unto Himself on the evening of an autumn day, October 1582.'[1]

> Ever the richest tenderest glow
> Sets round the autumnal sun—
> But there sight fails ; no heart may know
> The bliss when life is done.[2]

The room where Teresa was born is now a chapel, richly decorated, attached to the church dedicated to Nuestra Serafica Madre Santa Teresa de Jesus. Over the altar is a statue of the saint in ecstasy. The artist[3] has selected the moment when in a vision she beheld the Lord suffering grief and scorn—wounded for her transgressions—and when her soul was filled with anguish and remorse. The site of the garden where she and her brother formed hermitages, in which they might dwell in prayer and solitude, is still shown. Among her relics is a small ivory figure, representing the Saviour scourged, which is placed on the altar ; the rosary and staff used by Teresa are also carefully preserved.

But the decree which in 1836 abolished all the monasteries for men in Spain reduced also the number of nunneries, and the convent adjoining the church, which was erected in honour of Teresa's home, has shared the evil fortune of the day ; only a few secularised Carmelites remain to serve the offices of the church, which is still the glory of Avila.

---

[1] See *Histoire de Sainte Thérèse*, note, p. 433.

[2] Keble's *Christian Year* (Second Sunday after Epiphany).

[3] Hernandez.

In the Monastery of St. Joseph, on August 24, there is still an annual commemoration of the reform established by Teresa dating from this day. The clergy of the cathedral officiate, and the singing of Spanish airs after the mass by the Carmelite nuns is described as one of the most touching parts of the ceremony. On this anniversary also a picture of Teresa is carried in procession to all the cells to remind the nuns of their foundress ; and old-fashioned instruments, in use in her day—tambourines and timbrels— are played by four novices in memory of the first four orphans who were adopted by Teresa.

The body of Teresa was interred at first in the Carmelite convent at Alba de Tormes, but after a while was removed from thence to St. Joseph's at Avila ; finally, however, by a decree of Pope Sixtus V. the body of the saint was brought back to Alba, and her humble desire fulfilled, that 'a little corner of earth' should be there allowed her.

In the Convent of the Incarnation the chapel continues to this day unaltered. The stalls for the nuns are regarded with veneration as having been occupied in turn by Teresa, and in that which was reserved for her as prioress, a wooden statue is placed, representing her with her hand on the breviary, giving the signal for the office to commence.

The parlour of the convent also remains as in those days when visitors were permitted to flock in, and when Teresa's ready wit and powers of conversation charmed all who came.[1]

By the earnest request of the Spanish Church and nation Teresa was canonised in 1622 by Pope Gregory XV. at the same time as Isidore the labourer, Ignatius Loyola, Francis Xavier, and Philip Neri.

See *Souvenirs du Pays de Sainte Thérèse* (Abbé Plasse).

DIEGO, DE ESTELLA.

B. 1524.   D. 1598.[1]

'Who possesseth much ?   Even he that desireth little.'

'Kill thine enemy, *Sin,* when he is yet but little; for when he is grown up to his full size, for sparing him, he will murder thee.'

'As ashes do keep and preserve the fire, so doth humility preserve the grace of the Holy Ghost.'

'Happy is he who seeketh with his whole soul the love of God and things invisible ; he exchanges small for great, transitory for eternal, vile for precious, base for glorious, miserable for most comfortable, sour for sweet, and, in a word, nothing for all things.'

'There are certain precious stones which if they touch some metals lose their virtue, whilst, again, by contact with others their virtue increaseth.   Now love, being a most precious stone, doth lose its virtue if fastened upon thyself, but if fixed upon God, it groweth and increaseth mightily.'

'It is the custom of those who are appointed to be judges in single combats to measure the weapons of those who are to fight together in the lists.   So God, Who is the righteous Judge, doth take just measure of our spiritual weapons, and will not suffer us to be tempted above that we are able to bear.'

'He that snuffeth the candle with his bare fingers defileth his fingers, but the candle burneth the brighter thereby.   So he which decryeth and defameth the good man defileth his own soul and conscience, but the good man shines all the more brightly in God's sight.'

[1] M. Rousselot, in *Les Mystiques espagnols,* gives 1598 as the date of death of Diego de Estella.   Ticknor gives 1578.

'One of the plagues of Egypt was the plague of frogs, and one of the plagues of the world is the plague of evil speakers ; they sit like frogs all day in the mire of their own sinfulness, and when it waxeth dark croak out with a loud voice their neighbours' defects.'

'God made not thy tongue of bone, nor of any other hard substance, but of tender flesh, to put thee in mind that thy words should be gentle and soft, and not rough or sharp.'

'If thou wouldest enjoy the sweetness of prayer and be refreshed by heavenly contemplation, thou must lift up the whole force of thy will unto God. Some exercise themselves only in the intellectual part of the will, and not in that part which toucheth the affections. Such seek not to be enkindled with the love of God, but rather to attain some hidden knowledge of the nature of God ; therefore they occupy themselves in pondering in what manner our Lord was born, in what manner He subsisted, in what manner He suffered, in what manner He rose again from he dead, and other such like considerations, supposing that in such inquiries the contemplative life consists. But true contemplation consisteth not in speculations concerning these mysteries of the Divine Being, but in fixing the anchor of thy thoughts in the deep sea of God's infinite love to man, with whom in heart and mind thou must be united and incorporated, so as by and through His love to be purified and perfected.'

'Ever regard it as lost time curiously to remark what men say of thee.'

'Let not thy personal beauty puff thee up, and be not enamoured with the vain shadow thereof, lest thou fall into destruction and lose thy life, as did Narcissus by contemplation of his beauty. Remember that Absalom's goodly locks of hair served but as a halter to hang himself.

. . . .

'Abide not in the contemplation of the outward bark, but rather consider the root ; and labour to beautify and adorn thy soul, for all other beauty is but vain, corruptible, and transitory, which time consumeth and bringeth to naught.'

St. Luke—' *Did not our hearts burn within us whilst He talked with us by the way, and opened unto us the Scriptures ?* ' 'Thine heart will be well disposed to receive the print of the image of the Eternal King if thou dost warm and soften it with the heat of God's own Word.'

' The beasts of the field which God created for the earth do carry their heads downwards, and go on all fours, looking always towards the ground ; but man, created for heaven, standeth upright, that he may look heavenward and not downward, minding earthly things.'

———•◦•———

Diego de Estella was born in Portugal,[1] but his parents were natives of Navarre. He entered the order of St. Francis, and was a noted orator in his day, and confessor to the celebrated Anthony Perrenot, Bishop of Arras, afterwards known as Cardinal Granvelle.

Little has come down to us relating to Estella, or Stella, as he is sometimes called. It is said by Schottus that he became a Bishop, but this is discredited by Nicholas Antonio.

There is great divergence with regard to the date of his death. He wrote a Latin commentary on the Gospel of St. Luke, which appeared in 1578, having been published at Alcala ; but, like many other works of devotion in the sixteenth century, it was immediately placed on the Roman ' Index,' and was severely censured by many Spanish theo-

[1] The kingdom of Portugal was seized by Philip II. and annexed to Spain in 1580.

logians. It, however, appeared again in an amended form in
1582 from the Venetian press. His work on 'The Vanity
of the World' was written in the vernacular, and went
through several editions; but that which has made his name
as a devotional writer, and which has stamped him as a
Spanish Mystic, is his 'Meditation on the Love of God,'
which was also composed in Spanish, and which has been
translated into several languages. This work was highly
appreciated by Saint François de Sales, who himself wrote
a treatise bearing the same title.

It strikes the reader as incongruous that so saintly a
man should have been the director of the conscience of
one so infamous as Cardinal Granvelle. How long he remained in that position is not known, and it's probable
that he never accompanied the Cardinal to the Netherlands,
where his worst acts were committed.

Note.—Anthony Perrenot (famous as Cardinal Granvelle)
was a native of Burgundy. His father was a favourite with
Charles V., and the son became likewise the trusted servant
and adviser of the Emperor. His natural talents were early
developed. He possessed a vast amount of learning, and
had acquired a habit of observation which gave him quick
insight into the character of the men with whom he came
in contact. He entered the ecclesiastical state, and through
the court interest of his father was elevated at an early age
to the Bishopric of Arras. He was afterwards made Archbishop of Mechlin, in virtue of which appointment he became Primate of the Netherlands.

In 1561 Pope Pius IV. gave him a cardinal's hat.
Granvelle is described by his biographers as 'selfish, crafty,
and unscrupulous,' and whilst feigning complete subservience
obtained absolute mastery over his superiors. He stood
high in the counsels of Philip II., whose cold calculating
brain brooded long and silently over his sinister designs—

designs which were hatched into being, and became terrible
realities under the vigorous agency of his minister. Granvelle was at the head of both civil and ecclesiastical affairs
in the country, and through his instrumentality the Inquisition was established in the Netherlands. The laws against
heresy which had lain dormant during the first two years of
Philip's reign were enforced with remorseless severity. The
prisons were crowded, and every week men laid down their
lives for conscience' sake.

Granvelle had at first been the trusted adviser of the
Regent Margaret of Parma; he had also ingratiated himself
with the Flemish nobles; Orange and Egmont both regarded
him for a time with favour, but in the end he became so
distrusted and detested by all estates of men in the Netherlands that Philip was forced to recall him. In 1564, to the
joy of all men, the Cardinal took leave of Brussels, never
more to return.[1]

JUAN DE LOS ANGELOS.

FLOURISHED ABOUT 1540–70.

'The Name of Christ illumines, for He is the true Light
which illumines every man. There is nothing which arrests
the vehemence of a man's wrath, nothing which abates the
swelling of his pride, nothing which sustains the soul in
weariness, which restrains the flow of luxury, which tempers
the thirst of avarice, and puts to flight all unseemly things
like the preaching of the Name of Jesus.

'The very thought of Jesus brings peace; nothing so
comforts the spirit, nothing so heals, nothing so strengthens
the soul in goodness and holiness and chaste affection, as
meditation on the life and death of Jesus. All spiritual
life is dried up if not anointed with this oil, and without
savour if not salted with this salt.'[2]

---

[1] See *Dutch Republic* (Motley), and *Don John of Austria* (Sir
William Stirling Maxwell).

[2] On the Canticles (John of the Angels).

Juan flourished about the middle of the sixteenth century, and was the contemporary and friend of Francis Borgia, the well-known saint of the Jesuit order. But little is known of the history of Juan, beyond the fact that he belonged to the Franciscan order, and was the confessor of the Infanta Juana, the daughter of Charles V., who was Princess Regent of Spain during the last year of her father's reign, and the first years of the reign of her brother Philip II.

Juan belonged to the school of Spanish Mystics. He became Provincial of the Franciscan order, and it was probably through his influence that the Princess Juana founded the nunnery of barefooted Franciscans at Madrid, to which she retired at the age of twenty-three on resigning the Regency of Spain.[1]

LUIS PONCE DE LEON.

B. 1528. D. 1591.

'Patience does not consist in insensibility to pain nor in silent repression of grief, but in its uncomplaining endurance in the spirit of loving obedience.'

'It is an acknowledged truth that whilst the testator yet lives the will or testament is of no effect ; therefore Thou, O my God, in Thy bounteous generosity didst *give Thyself to die* that all might be fulfilled.'

[1] Juana was married when seventeen to her cousin Juan, Prince of Brazil, heir-apparent to the crown of Portugal—the only son of John III. and of Catherine, the sister of Charles V. After thirteen months of happy married life Prince Juan died, leaving his wife pregnant. To the joy of the whole nation a son was born in whom were centred the hopes of the Portuguese, and whose romantic history has made the name of Sebastian dear to his countrymen. In 1578 Don Sebastian was killed in battle by the Barbary Moors at the age of twenty-four, and ere long Portugal fell under the dominion of Philip II.

'The best and truest science is to know much of Christ, and verily this is the most high and the most Divine of all sciences. To understand this is to understand all the treasures of God's wisdom and knowledge which (in the words of St. Paul) "are hid in Him." It is to comprehend God's infinite love to man, His greatness, His majesty, His power, and the fulness of those glorious perfections which shine forth more especially in the mystery of Christ, the God-man. Now all, or the greater part, of these perfections would be better understood if we apprehended the meaning and force of those names which the Holy Spirit gives to Christ in Holy Scripture—names which are as abbreviations, wherein are hidden by God's Spirit all the marvels which it is possible for the human mind to receive.'

'To give way to vice is to degrade oneself, and descend step by step, till one falls into absolute nothingness.'

'Who, Holy Lord, that has heard within his soul Thy harmonies will not be henceforth deaf to the discordant sounds of Earth?'

(On the harmony and order of the celestial bodies.)[1]

'Even if Reason could not prove it, and even if we could in no other way understand how gracious a thing is Peace, yet would this fair show of the Heavens over our heads and this harmony in all their manifold fires sufficiently bear witness to it. For what is it but Peace, or, indeed, a perfect image of Peace, that we now behold and that fills us with such deep joy?

'Since, if Peace is, as St. Augustine with the beauty of truth declares it to be, *a quiet order or the maintenance of a well-regulated tranquillity in whatever order demands*, then what we now witness is surely its true and faithful image. For while these hosts of stars, arranged and divided into their several bands, shine with such surpassing splendour, and while each one of their multitude inviolably maintains

---

[1] *Names of Christ*, Christ as the Prince of Peace (Luis de Leon).

its separate station, neither pressing into the place of that next to it, nor disturbing the movements of any other, nor forgetting its own, none breaking the Eternal and Holy Law which God has imposed on it, but *all rather bound in one brotherhood, ministering one to another and reflecting their light one to another*, they do surely show forth *a mutual love* and as it were *a mutual reverence*, tempering each other's brightness and strength into *a peaceful unity and power*, whereby all their different influences are combined into one holy and mighty Harmony, universal and everlasting.

'And therefore may it be truly said not only that they do all form *a fair and perfect model of Peace*, but that they all set forth and announce in clear and gracious words what excellent things Peace contains within herself, and carries abroad whithersoever her power extends.'[1]

———◆◇◆———

Luis Ponce de Leon was born at Belmonte, in La Mancha,[2] and was of an old and distinguished family. His father was attached to the Spanish Court, but Luis manifested at an early age such a decided inclination for the cloister that his wishes were not opposed by his father. On leaving Valladolid, where his education had commenced, Luis was sent to Salamanca to study scholastic theology. His course was brilliant, and it was at this university that he acquired his first knowledge of Hebrew and other learned languages, in which he afterwards became so proficient. From Salamanca he went to Alcala, where, in spite of the persecutions which assailed the most distinguished of its professors, Biblical learning was at its height, and Luis de Leon turned with eager delight from the dryness of scholastic theology to the study of the Living Word in the original tongues. At seventeen years old he entered the

[1] See *History of Spanish Literature* (Ticknor).

[2] See *Mystiques espagnols* (Paul Rousselot). Ticknor, however, names Granada as the birthplace of Luis.

order of St. Augustine, to which Luther had belonged, and the course of Luis de Leon's life was thenceforth fixed; 'he never ceased to be a monk, and he never ceased to be attached to the university where he was bred.'[1]

In 1560 he became doctor of divinity, and two years afterwards, when only thirty-four years of age, he was raised to the chair of St. Thomas Aquinas at Salamanca, an honour which he won for himself in public competition, and which excited much enmity against him, especially from the rival order of St. Dominic. Luis was deservedly regarded as one of the most illustrious masters in the University of Salamanca; he was not only profoundly versed in several learned languages, but he had also made himself acquainted with art and science. Distinguished as a scholar and as a linguist, he was also distinguished as a Spanish Mystic. He had been a disciple of Luis de Granada, who had early instructed him in the mysteries of the spiritual life, and imbued him with that mysticism which opposed itself to the formalism of the age. Its aim was nothing less than 'a *re-formation* of the inner man by the unfettered movement of the Spirit of God within the soul.'[2] Men were no longer to rest in the outer camp, but, filled with spiritual unction, they were to enter within the veil, into that close vital union with the Lord in which is the perfection of worship. This was the theology of the Spanish Mystics, and it was the secret of that intense devotion which marked their lives.

In 1572 Luis de Leon was appointed to the chair of Sacred Literature; this afforded him full scope for the researches in which he delighted, both as a devout man and

[1] See *History of Spanish Literature* (Ticknor).
[2] See *Revue germanique* (1 janvier, 1863), *Etude sur Fray Luis de Leon* (M. Guardia).

a scholar, and he threw himself with enthusiastic ardour into the critical interpretation of the Scriptures. The influence of Luis over his auditors was immense ; his words struck a sympathetic chord in their hearts and at the same time aroused their intelligence. So remarkable was his gift of utterance that he went by the name of 'the Christian Cicero.' His courage equalled his eloquence, and he boldly used his oratorical powers to denounce ignorance and pride as the two great crying evils of the age. His views on intellectual culture were far in advance of those of most of his contemporaries ; he held ignorance to be inimical to the true faith—a discredit to the Church, and he regarded as a scandal the presumption of those who, disdaining the study of the sacred writings, yet as '*maestros teologos*' arrogated to themselves the right of instructing the people.[1] The popularity of Luis grew mightily, and the jealousy and suspicion of the secular clergy was aroused. His Biblical learning was an offence to them ; his regard for Rabbinical interpretations of Scripture proved, they said, that he was of Hebrew blood ; and when in his lectures he upheld Biblical criticism as serving to elucidate the text ('many significations being inclosed in the simplicity of one and the same thought'), and advocated a fresh translation of the sacred Scriptures, their animosity at once detected *Lutheranism* in his teaching. His enemies were on the watch, and ere long, through the treachery of a servant, it was discovered that, at the request of a friend, he had made a translation of the Canticles into the vernacular, to which he had added a commentary. This at once brought him within the grasp of his enemies—all such productions being contrary to an edict of the Holy Office. He was denounced to the tribunal of the Inquisition, and cast into prison.

[1] See *Mystiques espagnols* (Paul Rousselot).

To accuse a man of heresy was to destroy him, and the great theologian, the fearless professor, would doubtless have perished, but for his marvellous energy and presence of mind. All men trembled before that fearful engine of domination. Absolute obedience was enforced, and, inflexible in rigour, it crushed alike those whom it suspected of heresy, and those who ventured to assert any intellectual freedom ;[1] 'the human mind was held captive, weighed down by the chains of intolerance.' All who laboured to raise the minds of men out of the moral lethargy into which they had fallen, and to win them to a higher and spiritual life, knew the perils which beset their path ; the wheel and the faggot would probably have to be confronted if the charge of heresy could be fastened upon them.[2]

The courage and freedom of thought of Luis de Leon, joined to the frankness of his nature, exposed him to dangers already foreseen by Teresa of Avila, when she warned Gratian, the Provincial of her new order, ' Be very careful as to what you say in your preaching.'

In his criticisms on the translations of the Bible, Luis rested on this principle—that the translators were merely interpreters, not prophets ; their work was a human work, consequently not absolutely perfect.

The Council of Trent had declared that the Vulgate contained no errors, and had approved of it as the best translation existing, and the only one to be used by the Church. Luis fully admitted that it was neither erroneous nor falsified, if by these terms it was understood that the translators had not wilfully put therein anything erroneous ; but if, further than this, it was asserted that there were no

[1] See *Revue germanique* (*Etude sur Fray Luis de Leon*, M.Guardia).
[2] See *History of Spanish Literature* (Ticknor), and *Cloister Life of Charles V.* (Stirling).

H

passages altered, through the carelessness of copyists or edi-
tors, and that the Vulgate was exempt alike from omissions
and interpolations, he hesitated not to affirm that it had
many such defects. Several of these interpolations he had
pointed out to the Theologians of Louvain, through his friend
Arias Montanus,[1] as proving the need of revisal ; and in the
long list of accusations against Luis which followed, these
'offensive propositions,' as they were designated—were pro-
minently put forth as subversive of the faith of the Church.

In 1558 a brief had been granted by Pope Pius IV·
authorising the tribunals of the Inquisition to proceed
against all persons, lay and clerical, and of whatsoever rank,
supposed to be infected with the new belief—a power
which, taken in all its relations, was more formidable to the
progress of intellectual improvement than had ever before
been granted to any body of men, civil or ecclesiastical.[2]
In virtue of this brief, Cazalla, the favourite chaplain of the
Emperor Charles V., who for ten years had ministered to
him, was seized, and miserably put to death—some seven
months after the demise of his imperial master—with fourteen other 'heretics.'

The prisons became crowded with victims of all ranks.
Shepherds and muleteers, knights and noble ladies, were
associated in suffering, and died bravely—a noble band of
martyrs—at Valladolid, in October 1559, in the presence of
Philip II.[3]

Carranza also, Archbishop of Toledo, and Primate of
Spain, who had attended the Emperor on his deathbed,
was seized, and for eighteen years languished in captivity.

[1] See *Mystiques espagnols.*
[2] See *History of Spanish Literature* (Ticknor).
[3] See *Cloister Life of Charles V.* (Stirling). In 1781 the last
victim perished at the stake, and in 1808 the Inquisition was sup-
pressed in Spain.

'Thraldom of mind and heart was the aim of the Inquisition. Discipline and Formalism were employed to reduce
men to the state of mere lifeless machines.' [1]

Even in the solitude of the cloister 'an invisible eye'
pursued men, and marked not only their acts and words,
but even their supposed thoughts and intentions.

For five years Luis de Leon was imprisoned in the
dungeons of the Inquisition, having to answer interminable
interrogations. Innocence made him bold, and his faith
grew stronger under trial.

His sagacity and presence of mind never left him ; he
threaded his way through the darkest labyrinth without
stumbling. Alone, amid unknown accusers, and deprived of
all human aid, he clung with a firmer grasp to the hand of
the Divine Deliverer, and strength flowed into him from
that invisible touch. The consciousness of this vital union,
this Divine fellowship, sustained him, and enabled him with
consummate wisdom and perfect self-possession to avoid
the traps laid to entangle him, and to ward off the attacks of
his enemies. The delay in the final sentence was always a
point of calculation on the part of the Inquisitors, as a
means of wearing out the powers of mind and body of
the accused ; but Luis bore all with unfaltering patience.
' Meditation and prayer were his resource against the aridity
of controversy.' [2]

His one request on being arrested was that he might be
permitted to take with him to prison Luis de Granada's
' Treatise on Prayer,' and he protested afterwards that he
had learnt more from this little volume than from all the
theology of the schoolmen. Means were found secretly to
convey to him a Hebrew Bible, and in the study of the
Word of Life his soul received refreshment.

---

[1] See *Revue germanique* (*Etude sur Fray Luis de Leon*). [2] *Ibid.*

He found solace also in composing a work entitled ' The Names of Christ,' which he wrote—not in Latin for the sole benefit of the learned, but in Spanish—for the benefit of all Christian souls hungering after Divine Love and Truth. His expositions of the Book of Job, and of ' The Virtuous Woman ' in the Book of Proverbs, were likewise written during his captivity.

He was at length released, and when he reappeared with unsullied fame in his university, and was reinstated in the chair of Sacred Literature, before an assembly eager to hear and full of sympathy with his sufferings, he simply took up his theme where he had left off, five years before, beginning ' Deciamos ahora,' without a single allusion to himself, and as though all he had undergone had al- ready faded from his memory. He lived nearly fourteen years after his release, but his health never recovered the privations he had undergone in the cells of the In- quisition.

He died in 1591, engaged in the work of monastic reform, and at the head of his own order. Arias Montanus, the great Biblical scholar, was his intimate friend, and had likewise incurred the censure of the Holy Office, his works having been for a time under interdict. During the imprisonment of Luis de Leon he was falsely told that Arias was dead, with the hope that he would betray the views of his friend, whom the Inquisitors feared and wished to destroy. Luis de Leon is described as not only the best Hebrew critic and the most eloquent preacher, but also as the poet of Mysticism. His poems were not published till after his death, but they were regarded as masterpieces by Cervantes and Lope de Vega. A short time before his death, Luis de Leon commenced a life of Teresa of Avila, of which, how- ever, he was able to write little more than the preface.

In the cloister of the Augustinians at Salamanca, in what is called ' The Corner of Saints,' the body of Luis Ponce de Leon reposes.

PEDRO MALAN DE CHAIDE.

B. 1530.   D. 1592.

' There is no sinner, however fallen, in whom there is not *something* by which God can deliver him from the claws of the devil, if only he himself be willing to co-operate with God.'

' Man has salvation close at his hand, if he will but accept it.'

''The Eternal Father has begotten Him Who is the mirror of Himself, His Son, His Lamb, the express Image of His Person, in Whom dwells the fulness of His Being, and to Him He refuses nothing.'

' Where I cannot apprehend, I believe, reverence, and adore.'

Pedro Malan de Chaide was born at Cascante, in the province of Navarre.[1]   He was educated at the university of Salamanca, and was theological professor both at Saragossa and Huesca.   He entered the Augustinian order, and

---

[1] Navarre was annexed to Castile in 1512 by Ferdinand the Catholic, partly by force and partly by fraud ; the rightful heir, Jean d'Albret, being abandoned by his French allies, who profited by his ruin, as the territory was partitioned ; Ferdinand seizing all *south* of the Pyrenees, while the *northern* portion ultimately passed with Henri IV. to the Crown of France.   Pedro Malan de Chaide, therefore, was a Spaniard by birth.

belongs to the school of Spanish Mystics. Though a contemporary of St. Teresa, he does not seem to have known
her or to have been influenced by her writings.

He was popular as a preacher, and in his works rebukes
the formalism and irreligion of professing Christians. He
graphically describes the customs of the day, the corruption
and luxury which prevailed. 'Women present themselves
in God's sanctuary to attend mass, loaded with jewels,
bedizened as for a marriage, with more rings than fingers,
their faces with more colouring than the rainbow, and pros-
trate themselves before Him who was stripped, scourged,
crowned with thorns, nailed to the cross for their redemption. Men likewise, whose days are spent in folly and
dissipation, approach the confessional, followed by a page
bearing a cushion, on which the Hidalgo kneels for fear of
fatigue, and if the priestly confessor censures his dissolute
habits, he rises, exclaiming that a personage of his rank
cannot lead the life of a monk, and departs self-com-
placent.'

Such was the moral torpor into which Spain had fallen
in the sixteenth century, under the tutelage of the Inquisition.

Pedro Malan de Chaide's treatise on 'Divine Love, or
the Conversion of the Magdalen,' is a representation of the
soul which has sinned and forgotten God; and the love of
Christ shed abroad in the heart is shown to be the life-giving
power which overcomes sin.

This work was not published till after his death in 1592,
though the prologue was written some years earlier. He
was a poet of some merit, and 'The Conversion of the
Magdalen' contains some of his verses. Ticknor says of
this work that it is 'written with so much richness of language, and is often so eloquent, that it was much read when

it first appeared, and has not, even in recent times, ceased to be reprinted and admired.[1]

Malan de Chaide and Luis de Leon were of the same order; both were Augustinians, both belonged to the University of Salamanca; they had also another point of union —both of them upheld the use of the Spanish language in preaching and writing in preference to the Latin. Malan de Chaide declared that to write in the vernacular was no innovation, but a return to primitive custom, 'for in what tongue,' he asks, 'spake and wrote Moses and the prophets? Plato and Aristotle wrote in their vernacular, why should theologians be denied the licence conceded to philosophers?' He goes on indignantly to demand 'whether it could be regarded as just that those who were ignorant of Latin should be deprived of the help of religious books written in their native tongue. The most impure Spanish romances and poems were to be found in the pocket of every young girl. Was the Spanish language only to be used for works of extravagance and folly, such as "Amadis of Gaul," &c.? What were such pernicious books in the hands of the young, but like a knife in the hands of a fool?'

It is easy to understand why words of such freedom, such severe reprehension of the spirit of the age, were kept locked in the portfolio of the writer, and only saw the light when he was no longer under dread of the familiars of the Holy Office.

[1] *History of Spanish Literature.*

ST. JUAN DE LA CRUZ.

B. 1542.   D. 1591.

'Faith is the handmaiden who introduces us to the throne of the Lord.'

'All our goodness is *a loan*; God is the owner.'

'God *reigns* only in that soul which is tranquil and devoid of self-seeking.'

'He who through distraction loses the thread of his prayer, is like one who lets a bird escape which he held in his hand.   He will recover it with difficulty.'

'As a man dragging a heavily laden cart up hill, so is that soul on its way to God which does not deny self and cast aside the cares of this life.'

'Earthly desires are to the soul like the suckers which sprout from the tree; they sap its strength and destroy its fertility.'

'Our anxiety *to possess* impoverishes us more than the want of things.'

'Do not be depressed by all the evil that happens in the world, for you know not the good which God will extract from it.'

'When the soul seeks consolation *from God only*, God is ready at once to bestow it.'

'As we clothe with garments the poor and naked one, so the Lord will clothe and adorn with His purity, His meekness, and His spirit, the soul which has stripped itself of its passions and desires.'

'He who obeys not his passions will mount readily in spirit towards God; even as a bird flies freely which has its wings unclipped.'

'It is certain that not to advance in the spiritual life by

overcoming self is to fall back, and not to increase is to lose even that which we formerly possessed.'

'It matters not whether the wire which holds the bird be thick or slight, since it equally prevents its taking wing ; so likewise is it of no moment whether the sin which holds us captive be great or small, since it equally prevents the soul's rising towards perfection and union with God.'

'We must not seek to adjust our trials to ourselves, but we must adjust ourselves to our trials.'

'When a vessel is full of liquid the least crack suffices, unless it be stopped, to let every drop leak out ; so if the soul, however filled with virtue and grace, close not up the aperture which a little sin has made, grace will ooze out little by little until all is spent.'

'Accept as a fact throughout your religious life that you are to be shaped, chiselled, and polished through the medium of others ; look therefore upon all persons as instruments of God to train you by divers ways, and consider this training (ofttimes grievous) as designed to make you holy.'

'As the sun, rising in the morning, shines into thy house if thou dost but open thy windows, so God, the unsleeping King, will shine in upon the soul which unfolds itself to Him ; for God, like the sun above us, is ready to enter within each of us if we open unto Him.'

Canticles v. 8. ' *Tell Him.*'

'The soul here does no more than represent its necessities to the Beloved ; for he who loves wisely is not eager *to ask* for that which he wants or desires ; he is satisfied with simply making known his necessities, so that the Beloved may do what shall seem to Him good. Thus the Blessed Virgin at the marriage feast of Cana asked not of her Divine Son, but meekly told Him " *They have no wine* ; " so also the sisters of Lazarus sent to our Lord not to implore Him to heal their brother, but only to say, " *Lord, behold he whom Thou lovest is sick.*"

' *Come, O south wind, thou that awakenest love*' (Canticles).

' By the south wind is here meant the Holy Ghost, who
awakeneth love ; for when the Divine Breath breathes into
the soul, it so influences and refreshes it, that it may truly be
said to quicken or awaken the love which before lay dead
or asleep.'

———◦◇◦———

The name of Juan de la Cruz will ever be associated
with that of Teresa of Avila, by whom he is described as
' one of the purest souls in the Church of God.'   He was
undoubtedly the most remarkable among the friars of her
Reformed order, and ranks high in the school of Spanish
Mystics.   His family history is not without its romance.

His father, Gonzalez de Yepez, belonged to an ancient
Castilian race, boasting the purest Spanish blood.   Gonzalez
lived with a rich uncle in the city of Toledo, and seemed
destined to a brilliant fortune.   But all his worldly prospects
were ruined by his marriage with Catarina Alvarez, a poor
village girl endowed only with great beauty.   By this step
he forfeited the support and regard of his proud relations,
who at once and for ever cast him off; but he had great
happiness in the love of his lowly-born wife, and never
regretted the sacrifice he had made for her sake.

They lived in the little hamlet of Fontiveros, lying
between Salamanca and Medina del Campo.   It was
Catarina's native village, and there Gonzalez worked with
his hands for their daily bread, following the trade of a
weaver.   Three sons were born to them.   After the birth of
Juan, the third child, and the subject of this sketch, Gonzalez
sickened and died, leaving his wife and children without
means of support.   Catarina, widowed and destitute, removed
to Medina del Campo, a thriving commercial town, where she
hoped to procure work more easily than in her native village.

Here her distress became known to a benevolent man named Alvarez. He was no relation to her, though bearing the same name. Through his kindness Juan was placed in a hospital at Medina, to which his protector devoted his time and his fortune. Alvarez took a deep interest in the boy, and was pleased with the evident joy it gave him to be allowed to help in waiting on the sick and infirm. He sent him afterwards to the Jesuits' College for his education, and when old enough to choose a profession, Alvarez purposed that he should become chaplain of the hospital; but this was not to be Juan's vocation.

When he was about to receive minor orders he told his protector that he felt irresistibly drawn to the monastic life. A Divine Voice, which he believed he had heard in prayer, had already called him to be the reformer of an ancient order, and his one desire was to live under the strictest religious rule, in complete renunciation of the world. He accordingly, at the age of twenty-one, offered himself as a lay brother to the Carmelite friars of St. Anne at Medina del Campo. He was received, and was sent soon after to the University of Salamanca to complete his religious education. He had great talent, and the success which attended his career at the University would have been gratifying to most men. In Biblical knowledge and theology he had been especially distinguished. But academical triumphs gave no pleasure to Juan, rather were they distasteful to his sensitive nature. He cared only to have the testimony *within* that God was well pleased, and he gladly turned away from the distracting praise of men to the seclusion of the Carmelite convent. He made his profession as a friar in 1564. From henceforth the Scriptures and the works of the early Fathers were his chief study, and his one aim was to promote a higher religious tone among his brethren. His fervour and ardent zeal induced him to adopt the primitive Carmelite rule in all its austerity, but the laxity and indifference of his brother friars baffled all his endeavours after reform. The flame of Divine love which burnt brightly within his own soul had apparently kindled no warmth in others ; and he, who had thought himself set for the revival of spiritual life in his order, felt chilled and disheartened by the coldness with which he was met. One man alone during these three years had evinced any sympathy with Juan ; this was the prior of the convent, Antonio de Heredia. He had long been disquieted by the laxity of discipline which prevailed in the convent, and he had tried in vain to bring about a change, for Heredia himself earnestly desired to lead a life of closer consecration. The fervour of Juan had powerfully stirred his mind, and the two friends, animated by the same desire and hopeless of effecting any reform among their brethren, decided to withdraw from the Carmelites and to seek admission into the more rigid order of the Carthusians.

It was the turning-point in their lives, for at this juncture (1567) they met for the first time Teresa of Avila, who was passing through Medina del Campo to inspect another monastery. Teresa was now fifty-two years old, Juan twenty-five. He was preparing for priest's orders, and the ascetic monk—full of intelligence and religious ardour, feeble in body but strong in spirit, seeking a stricter rule and a life of greater mortification—at once made a profound impression upon Teresa. She had heard of him already, but when she saw him she felt that she had met a kindred spirit, a soul on fire with the love of God. Surely this was the man of whom she was in quest, who was to accomplish her reform ! In spite of his youth she never doubted for a moment his fitness, and he at once promised to be her first friar, on condition that 'she did not make him wait too long.'[1]

In the following year (1568) the first monastery of men of the Reformed Carmelite rule was established 'for him, and by him' at Durvelo. Here he was, after two months, joined by his friend, Antonio de Heredia, who had resigned the office of Prior at Medina.

The ardent heart of Juan was lifted up in praise and thanksgiving. He had clung with unswerving faith to his early conviction that the Voice he had heard in prayer was none other than the Voice of God. This belief had shaped his course in life ; it had stimulated his zeal and sustained him in disappointment. And now the appointed time had come, and the word spoken to his inward ear in his boyhood was about to be fulfilled.

Durvelo was a retired hamlet, lying between Medina and Avila, where a small farmhouse had been placed at Teresa's disposal, to be used as a monastery for her Discalced friars. Nothing could exceed the wretchedness of the place. Teresa had gone to inspect it, and she sighed as she thought of Heredia. How could the worthy Prior, no longer young, and weak in health, accustomed to his clean cell, and the company of his books, endure to live in so squalid a dwelling ? But both Heredia and Juan at once agreed to take possession, and in Advent 1568 the first mass was said in the porch of the building, now converted into a church. Two low cabins filled with straw were their only shelter at night. And—

> As of old, by two and two
> His herald Saints the Saviour sent—

so from the hut of Durvelo these first two friars of the Reformed rule went forth, day by day, preaching the Gospel

[1] See *Les Mystiques espagnols* (Rousselot), and *Life of Saint Teresa.*

of Christ to the neighbouring peasants. In the winter they
often walked many leagues barefooted through the snow
to reach some distant hamlet. They sought out the simple
and rude, the untaught and the ignorant, and gathered them
together to hear the Word. They disregarded hardships,
for, in all their labours, they were possessed with the courage
and enthusiasm of men working for One whom they knew
and loved.

Teresa visited them in the following Lent on her way to
Toledo. She arrived unexpectedly, and found Fra Antonio
busily sweeping the floor of their little church. 'What is
this, father?' she exclaimed. 'What has become of your
dignity?' 'I hate the day when I had any,' was his re-
joinder.

In 1570 the two friends removed to Mancera, where a
church and a small monastery had been built for Discalced
Carmelites.

The excessive austerities they practised somewhat disturbed Teresa. She thought that their self-imposed penances might impede their usefulness. But she found it
always more difficult to control her friars than her nuns;
and, as the number of these religious establishments gradually increased, she sorrowfully admitted that it was more
easy to turn haughty Castilians into heroes and martyrs,
than to mould them into peaceful and submissive saints.
These two first friars of her order, however, were to her a
never-failing source of consolation : sharing with her every
burden, following where she led, often hindered like herself
in their labours of love, and persecuted by the Mitigated
Carmelites with all the greater animosity, because they had
forsaken them for Teresa's Reformed rule. When therefore,
in 1577, open hostility was declared by the Mitigated
Carmelites, these two men were the first to suffer. Both

were imprisoned, but on Juan was inflicted the severest treatment.

He had been appointed spiritual director of the nuns of the Incarnation at Avila, who, although they were not of the Reformed rule, had chosen Teresa as their Prioress. Juan lived with another friar in a small hermitage near the convent, keeping perfectly aloof from all disputes, and leading a life of prayer and contemplation. He did not attempt to force the Reformed rule upon others. His own desire was 'to make Christ as vividly real to all with whom he was brought in contact, as He was to his own soul.' For this he lived, and he had won the love and respect of all around him. But his holy self-denying life was a reproach to the unreformed friars, and at midnight the door of his cell was forced open ; he was seized and bound like a criminal ; all his papers were confiscated, and he himself dragged to a convent of Mitigated friars, where he was shut up and beaten. He was then removed to Toledo, where, for nine months, he was incarcerated in a close dark cell, so confined in space that he could hardly move or breathe for want of air, and which in the heat of summer became almost insupportable. He could not read for want of light ; he was fed on bread and water, and scourged thrice in the week. But, though his persecutors might starve him, he had meat to eat which they knew not of ; they could place him in darkness, but he had that inner light which cometh down from heaven ; so that, in his cruel captivity, he was able to say, 'The soul of one who serves God always swims in joy, always keeps holiday, always dwells in the palace of jubilation, ever singing, with fresh ardour and fresh pleasure, a new song of joy and love.'

At the expiration of nine months his escape was accomplished, and he took refuge in a Reformed monastery at

Almadovar.   After a time he became Superior of a small
convent in a desert place, far removed from any habitation, known as 'the Calvary.' ` In 1579 he founded the
Convent of Baeza for Discalced friars, and afterwards that of
Segovia.   Two years later he was made Prior of Granada,
and, in 1585, Vicar Provincial of Andalusia.

In 1591, having opposed some harsh measures of the
Chapter, he was treated with great cruelty—dismissed from
all his offices, and banished to the solitary convent of Peg-
nela in the Sierra Morena.   It was here that he wrote his
Mystical treatises—'The Obscure Night,' and the 'Ascent
of Mount Carmel.'   In the former he describes the spiritual
desolation through which he had passed.   In the language
of the Psalmist, 'the enemy persecuted his soul ; his life
was smitten down to the ground ; and he was laid in darkness as one long dead.'   The spirit of joy and gladness had
given place to the spirit of sadness, and 'his heart within
him was desolate.'   It is sad to read of his self-inflicted
penances.   He did not live long ; strength failed him ; he
was about to leave the body which he had treated with
such severity, and after four months of intense suffering, he
expired.   When he felt that death was at hand, he begged
to be left alone with one friar.   The Crucifix was in his
hand, which he kissed repeatedly.   Light gleamed in upon
his darkness, the spirit of heaviness was exchanged for that
of praise, and a Divine calm and peace again filled his soul.

He turned to his companion, and, with a radiant look
upon his face, said, 'Believe me, brother, the love of God
makes death welcome, and most sweet to a soul.'   He had
come to the water's edge, the dark river lay before him, but
he looked to the shore beyond, where there was no darkness
to dismay him, but the light of the glory of God to rejoice
his soul.

About nine in the evening, after receiving the last Sacra-ments, he inquired the hour, and, on being told, exclaimed with joyful accents, 'Blessed be God, the next matins will be in heaven !'

He begged to have the Psalms read to him. The friars now returned to his cell, and asked for his pardon and blessing. 'I am no longer your Superior,' was his reply; 'it is not for me to bless.' But, on their entreaties and the command of the Superior, he made the sign of the Cross, and blessed them. At midnight he passed away, his last words being, 'Into Thy hands I commend my spirit.'[1]

JUAN FALCONI.

B. 1596. D. 1638.

'If you were to give a diamond to your friend, and had once placed it in his hands, you would not say, and reiterate day after day, that you give him this ring, that you make him a present of it; you would simply leave it in his hands, never recalling your gift, because as long as you do not withdraw it, and have no thought or desire to do so, it is a present which you have made him and which you do not revoke. So in like manner, when once you have given yourself absolutely into the Hands of our Lord by a loving Self-surrender, you have only to abide there. Refrain from disquietude, from all strenuous effort to make fresh acts of Surrender, and from all attempt to increase sensible emotion.

'These only disturb the godly simplicity of the Spiritual Act already performed by your Will. That which is most important is this—*not to take away from God that which you have given to Him.*'

[1] *Vie de Saint Jean de la Croix*, par le R. P. Dorothée de Saint Alexis.

I

Juan Falconi was born at Fifiana, in Spain. He entered the order of 'Our Lady of Mercy,' founded in the thirteenth century by San Pedro Nolasco for the redemption of slaves and captives. He was a Mystic writer, a man of most devout life, whose works have been translated from the Spanish into French, Italian, and German. His chief work is entitled, in Italian, 'Alphabeto per saper leggere in Christo.'

MIGUEL DE MOLINOS.[1]

B. 1627. D. 1696.

'It is certain that our Lord Jesus Christ is the Guide, the Door, and the Way. And before the soul can be fit to enter into the Presence of the Divinity, and to be united with the Divine Nature, it must be washed with the precious Blood of the Redeemer, and adorned with the rich robes of His Passion. . . .

'Let the soul, then, when it would enter into recollectedness, place itself at the gate of Divine Mercy, which is the sweet and blessed remembrance of the Cross and Passion of the Word that was made Flesh, and died for the love of man. Let the soul stand there with humility, resigned to the Will of God in whatsoever it pleases the Divine Majesty to do with it . . . continuing silent and quiet in the Presence of the Lord.'

'The way of inward peace is in all things to be conformed to the pleasure and disposition of the Divine Will. . . . This conformity is the sweet yoke that introduces us into the regions of internal peace and serenity. Hence we may know that the rebellion of our will is the chief occasion of our disquiet, and that, because we will not submit to the

---

[1] Miguel de Molinos must not be confounded with *Luis Molina*, a Spanish Jesuit, born 1535, died 1600), whose followers were called *Molinists*. Those of Miguel de Molinos were called *Quietists*.

sweet yoke of the Divine Will, we suffer so many streights and perturbations.

'O soul! if we submitted our own to the Divine Will, and to all His disposition, what tranquillity should we feel! what sweet peace! what inward serenity! what supreme felicity and earnest of bliss!'

'Ever remember that thy soul is the Habitation and Kingdom of God. . . . If a man hath a safe fortress he is not disquieted, though his enemies pursue him, because by retreating within this fortress they are disappointed of their prey and overcome.

''The strong Castle that will enable thee to triumph over all thine enemies, visible and invisible, and over all snares and tribulations which may beset thee, *is thine own soul*, because within that soul dwells the Divine Aid and Sovereign Succour. Retreat within that sanctuary, and all will be quiet, secure, peaceable and calm. It should be thy chief and continual exercise to pacify thy heart, which is God's throne, that the Supreme King may rest therein. The way to pacify it is to enter within thyself by means of internal recollectedness. All thy safeguard is to be Prayer and a loving habitual recollection of the Divine Presence.'

'Would it not be deemed impertinent and disrespectful if, being in the presence of a king, thou shouldest every now and then say to him, "Sire, I believe your majesty is here present?" Surely it is the very same with regard to the Divine Presence? By the eye of pure faith the soul sees God, believes in Him, and is in His Presence, and therefore has no need *to say* "My God, Thou art here," but *to believe it*, and let Faith guide and conduct the soul onwards into contemplation.'

'Remember that it is always good to speak like one that learns, and not like one that knows.'

—●◇●—

Miguel de Molinos was a Spaniard of noble descent. His parents were rich and honourable, living at Minozzi, in the diocese of Saragossa in Aragon. Miguel was born on St. Thomas's Day, 1627. He was educated for the ecclesiastical state at the University of Coimbra in Portugal, where he took his theological degree.

He neither obtained nor sought any kind of preferment ; satisfied with priestly orders, he dedicated himself to the service of the Church without designing any advantage whatever to himself.

After a career of some distinction in his own country, where he had devoted much time to the study of the Scriptures and of the writings of St. Teresa and other Spanish Mystics, Molinos, unhappily for himself, went to Rome, where he acquired a wonderful popularity as a spiritual director, and introduced that mystical theology with which he was deeply imbued, and which had wrought such a spiritual revival in his own land. In Rome he led a blameless life, and was honoured as a man of great learning, piety, and disinterestedness. In 1675 he published a book entitled, 'Il Guida Spirituale.' Four members of the Inquisition and a Jesuit father named Esparsa (greatly esteemed at that time in Rome) gave the book their cordial approval. It had even the sanction of the Pope himself[1] and of his cardinals, and so popular did the 'Guida' become that in less than six years it had passed through twenty editions and had been translated into several languages. In Spain, where mysticism may be said to have been indigenous, the book met with especial favour. The reputation of Molinos was heightened and his influence extended by the success of his work. Many earnest and devout men in Rome resorted to him for spiritual counsel, and a great revival of

[1] Innocent XI. (Odescalchi).

religion followed his teaching. The key-note of his theology was 'the union of man's will with the Divine Will.'

It was no new theory. Ruysbröck and the German Mystics of the fourteenth century had taught the same truth, that the spiritual life is none other than a life of conscious union with God, and

> 'tis essential to this blest estate
> To keep the will within the Will Divine.[1]

Molinos dwelt much on the cultivation of a devout habit of mind—a spirit of contemplation and inward communion with the Unseen ; but he did not insist—as was customary with spiritual directors—on the practice of bodily mortification and a multiplicity of ceremonial observances.

His followers made no outward demonstration of increased devotion ; they led a more quiet retired life ; their works of charity were more abundant, but they were performed with greater secrecy. They raised no loud cry for reform ; but a deep silent movement was gathering strength day by day within the Church, and before long the Jesuits took alarm. The friendship of Molinos was sought by the most illustrious in Rome ; he was a frequent guest within the Vatican, and men from all parts of Europe who had read the 'Guida' corresponded with him. Among the religious orders none joined more heartily in his views than the fathers of the Oratory,[2] three of whom—Coloredi, Ciceri, and Petrucci—were his especial friends ; all these became cardinals. Many other members of the Sacred College courted him, but there was one above all the rest who sought the society of Molinos, and with whom he formed a close intimacy. This was Cardinal d'Estrées, a man of great learning and a doctor of the Sorbonne, who professed

---

[1] *Paradiso* (canto iii.)
[2] Founded by Saint Philip Neri.

himself eager to reform certain abuses which had crept
into the Roman Church. He was at that time the am-
bassador of Louis XIV. to the Papal Court, and he hoped,
by means of Molinos and through this higher teaching, to
free the Church from some superstitious practices which
were scoffed at by the world, and which he thought led
many into infidelity.

But there were other followers of Molinos led by a
different motive ; among these were priests and monks of
the different monastic orders, who sought through this 'new
method' to undermine the influence of the Jesuits and
check their aggressions.   Molinos in his ' Method' had
indeed asserted the need of a spiritual director, but he had
not enforced confession as necessary on all occasions before
partaking of the Holy Eucharist.   He pressed upon his
disciples of the *laity* the infinite *privilege* of *daily* communion as an inward application of the soul to Christ Himself
in the showing forth of His death in the Holy Sacrament.
But the only condition on which he insisted was ' *to be free
from mortal sin.*'   This at once struck a deadly blow at the
power wielded by the Jesuits in the confessional.

Thus threatened, the whole energy and sagacity of the
order was directed against the man whom they deemed
their opponent.   The ruin of Molinos was determined
upon.   Whispered reports to his disadvantage began to be
circulated ; he was said to be of Jewish race and to hold
some of the tenets of his early faith.   They did not venture
to attack him *openly*, his popularity being so great, but by
covert means they hoped to gain their ends.

For this purpose Father Segneri, a Jesuit of some
repute, was directed to compose a treatise on the principles
of *Quietism*, the name given to the teaching of Molinos.
Segneri took a dexterous mode of decrying the ' Guida.'

He began by insidious praise, greatly commending the book, and blaming those who had said anything to detract from its merit. He magnified the contemplative state as infinitely superior to all others, but very few, he said, were capable of attaining it. The 'Guida' was, therefore, a book for saints, not for ordinary mortals.

It enjoined a state of *passivity*, of absolute *quietude*, in which the soul neither reasons nor reflects, but simply *surrenders* itself to God and *receives*.

Who in this world of strife could hope to attain such abstractedness? For *a few moments*, indeed, it might be possible for *some few* to reach such an exalted state, but to suppose that it was open *to any man* to rise to this state of quietude was an error utterly to be deprecated. He proceeded to censure some of the expressions used in the 'Guida,' without, however, naming Molinos, and insisted that the *quietude* therein described was a favour from on high so rare and extraordinary that no humble-minded Christian would venture to ask it of God.

Segneri's treatise — evidently inspired by hatred of Molinos—was received with general indignation. It was brought before the Inquisition, and the author was condemned and his work placed on the 'Index' of prohibited books.

But this failure only increased the enmity of the Jesuits. They continued to inveigh against a system which tended, they said, to the subversion of all discipline, and a culpable neglect of appointed means of grace. These assertions made so much noise, and aroused such discussion, that at length the 'Guida' was brought under a new and closer scrutiny. There were, undoubtedly, passages in it liable to misconstruction; but Molinos and his devoted follower, Petrucci, having been examined by the Inquisitors, justified themselves so completely from all suspicion of heresy, that their accusers were again discomfited, and severely censured by the In- quisitors for their calumnious assertions. Petrucci, indeed, gained so much credit by his answers to the interrogations put to him, that he was made Bishop of Jessi by the Pope.

Foiled in their attempts, the Jesuits resolved to secure their object by other and more subtle means. Père la Chaise, a Jesuit, was at that time Confessor to Louis XIV., at once the most profligate, the most bigoted, and the most powerful sovereign in Europe. Pope Innocent XI. was known to regard with favour the Austro-Spanish party in Rome, which was opposed to France. The Jesuits were not slow to take advantage of this. It was easy to arouse the jealousy of the French king, who resented any policy, on the part of the Holy See, adverse to his own. With the view, therefore, of harassing the Pope, Père la Chaise, with consummate craft, incited his royal penitent to make it a formal reproach to the Holy See that, whilst he, the eldest son of the Church, was striving to extirpate heresy by purg- ing the soil of France from Jansenists and Huguenots, the Head of the Church was himself cherishing it in his own palace, by favouring and entertaining as an honoured guest one who was corrupting the doctrine, or at least the devotion, of that body of which he was the Sacred Head.

Innocent XI. was a man remarkable for his mildness and humility, and of great purity of life. He is described by Ranke as the first Pope who absolutely abstained from nepotism, fulfilling all the duties of his high office with in- flexible integrity.[1] He received the insulting address of the French king with much dignity and composure; but the audacity of the Jesuits, thus supported by Louis, knew no bounds. They affected to lament the blindness of the Pope

[1] See *Lives of the Popes* (Ranke).

and Cardinals, and openly denounced, as the most dangerous foe to the faith of Christendom, the man whose
reputation for sanctity had stood unblemished for twenty
years, and who had long enjoyed the friendship of the Head
of the Church.

To accomplish his ruin, the Jesuits dared at length to
question the orthodoxy of the Sovereign Pontiff. Even the·
triple crown could not shield the protector of Molinos from
suspicions of heresy, and Innocent, who had been elected,
like another St. Ambrose, by the acclamations of the people,
was now upbraided by the populace as a traitor to the faith.
Molinos was again summoned to appear before the Inqui
sition, but he defended himself with such skill and courage
that the accusations against him fell to the ground, and
were condemned as false and libellous.

To the dismay of the Jesuits at this time, another 'of
their society was found to support Molinos. This was Appiani, one of the most eminent men in the Roman College.
Esparsa had already been withdrawn from Rome. Appiani
was at once silenced by imprisonment. Treachery was then
employed to support fresh charges against the persecuted
Molinos. Orders were despatched from Versailles, requiring Cardinal d'Estrées to urge, with all possible vigour, the
prosecution of this enemy of the faith. D'Estrées did not
hesitate ; he obeyed the king, and sacrificed his friend.
There was no evidence against Molinos ; but D'Estrées, the
man in whom he trusted, who had been his familiar friend,
supplied the defect, and came forward as his accuser before
the Inquisition. He scrupled not to assert that he had
suspected Molinos of heresy from the first, and had only
sought his friendship to unmask his errors.

Molinos, true and loyal himself, had opened his heart
unreservedly to this man, and, through his instrumentality,

a correspondence on spiritual matters had been carried on
for many years with men of note in France.   All the letters
found in the possession of Molinos were seized and sifted to
extract some evidence against him.   It is said that 'sus-
picious documents' were discovered, and it is not impossible that in this vast correspondence [1] were found some
letters from Jansenist writers.

The views of the great Arnauld, as set forth in his work
on 'La Fréquente Communion,' differed widely from those
of Molinos, but we know that Molinos had read and con-
troverted some passages in Arnauld's book,[2] and he may
have interchanged letters with the Jansenist leader.

If such were the case, it would afford another weapon of
attack against the accused.

He was not permitted to speak in self-defence, and was
cast into prison,[3] where he lay for nearly two years without
trial.   The Pope was powerless to protect the man whom
he had thought of making a Cardinal ; but he sent Cardinal
Petrucci to visit him secretly ; what passed between them
did not transpire, but the Pope always maintained, in spite
of all the charges brought against Molinos, 'that, although
he might have erred in doctrine, his life was spotless.'   He
was almost forgotten by the multitude, when suddenly, in
1687, seventy of his followers were cast into the dungeons
of the Inquisition.   Their only crime was pursuing a method
of devotion which had once been lauded throughout Italy
as 'sublime.'

A circular letter was addressed to the Italian bishops,
apprising them 'that secret assemblies were held in their
dioceses, where inadmissible and dangerous errors were

---

[1] It is said that 20,000 letters were collected by the Inquisitors.

[2] See *Letter from Rome* (Bishop Burnet).

[3] May 1685, the year of the Revocation of the Edict of Nantes.

taught, under the pretence of inculcating higher experimental doctrines.' It was consequently enjoined upon them 'to forbid and disperse these assemblies, and to pursue to justice such as should be found adopting novelties, which the Catholic Church regarded as heretical and criminal.'

The prisons of the Holy Office were soon crowded with *Quietists.* It was sufficient for anyone to lead a retired life, to appear but seldom at confession, and he was immediately suspected ; and if the informer were an enemy, suspicion was soon followed by conviction.[1]

Among the suspected were men and women of high birth, good Churchmen, and great scholars.

The Count and Countess Vespiniani—personal friends of the Pope's nephew, Don Livio, Duke of Ceri—were seized and imprisoned, and he himself was not without fear of arrest. When summoned before the Inquisitors the Countess Vespiniani bravely defended herself. She said that 'it was to her confessor alone that she had spoken of her method of prayer; he therefore must have revealed what had been confided to him under the seal of confession. Who would confess if confession were made an engine of persecution, and placed you at the mercy of a betrayer? Henceforth she would confess to God alone.'[2]

Her bold words, joined to her high rank, produced effect, and the Inquisitors fearing to proceed further against them, she and her husband were released. Some of the accusations were that 'the Quietists did not lean as formerly on their directors for guidance, and some who were *laymen* and married, communicated *daily*—an ominous sign, daily communion being a privilege reserved for the clergy.'[3]

The Carmelites and other religious orders were com-

---

[1] See *Hours with the Mystics* (Vaughan).
[2] *Ibid.*   [3] *Ibid.*

manded to give up the 'Guida' and any other books of devotion of a similar character, and to resume the use of the Rosary, their former mechanical mode of prayer. The Inquisitors drew up nineteen articles from the ' Guida ' which they declared to be heretical. Every sort of infamous report was spread abroad against Molinos, branding him not only with heresy, but with impurity of life. These falsehoods were believed by the credulous Roman populace, so that when at length he was brought forth from his dungeon to receive the judgment of the Inquisition, the rage of the mob was so excited, that they shouted, ' Al fuoco, al fuoco ! ' and would themselves have torn him in pieces had he not been well guarded by the Sbirri. In order to secure a large attendance at the trial, and to give it as much as possible the appearance of a popular manifestation against the accused and his followers, it had been notified that plenary indulgence would be accorded to all who should assist at the ceremony.[1]

To all except the accused the day of trial was a fête day in Rome. The streets adjacent to the church of Santa Maria sopra Minerva were filled with an exultant populace. The church itself was thronged from an early hour with an eager crowd to hear the condemnation of a man long regarded with the deepest veneration. The stalls were filled by nobles and prelates. The Cardinals had special places on a raised daïs, and facing them sat the Grand Inquisitor, surrounded by the familiars of the Holy Office.

Once before the Minerva had been the scene of a notable trial. Within the walls of its convent Galileo had been constrained to give his famous repudiation of the truth he had discovered ; and now another victim was to be sacrificed to the tyranny and hatred of the Inquisition.

Dressed in priestly robes, with lighted taper thrust be-

[1] See *Molinos the Quietist* (Bigelow).

tween his chained hands, Molinos slowly walked to the place assigned to him. One of the Dominican fathers read aloud his accusation, and as each separate charge was heard the excited mob within and without the church, stirred to a frenzy of fanaticism, cried, 'Al fuoco, al fuoco !'

Through the long ceremony of excommunication, Molinos maintained his accustomed serenity. As he looked round on the crowd of infuriated faces, the only words he was heard to utter were, 'Infamato, ma pentito.' Some few greeted him sadly, to whom he meekly bowed in recognition. He was sentenced to be confined for life in the prison of the Holy Office.

With perfect tranquillity he entered the cell which he was to leave no more till death released him, calling it his '*piccola stanza*'—words which recall the saying of Tertullian, '*Away with the name of prison; let us call it a retirement.*'

Then turning to the priest who accompanied him, Molinos said, 'Addio, padre ! We shall meet again at the Day of Judgment, and then it will appear on which side is truth, whether on my side or on yours.'[1]

He lived nine years longer, and died on Holy Innocents' Day, December 28, 1696, in the seventieth year of his age.

How those nine years were passed, what suffering and cruelty he may have endured, can never be known.

A modern French writer, speaking of the Spanish Mystics recognised by the Church, says, 'If circumstances had permitted them, they would perhaps have sought to

---

[1] Reports were spread that he had abjured his opinions, but in an extant letter of Father Segneri, his Jesuit opponent, written after the trial, he deplores '*the obstinacy of the unhappy Molinos*' as '*the extreme of wickedness.*' Had Molinos abjured, Segneri would not have alluded to his *obstinacy*.

achieve more than the reform of their convents. We may suppose without improbability that their action would have been less circumscribed without the sombre supervision of the Inquisition. This very supervision seems to indicate it. . . . Had the Spanish Mystics been more free, they might have taken a wider range, without, however, abjuring Catholicism. . . . They would gladly have been reformers, though after the manner of St. Bernard. Most gladly would they have re-established the Church in her primitive purity, but without striking at her unity.

'Their ambition did not go beyond that of the monk of Clairvaux, who asked that "before dying, it might be given him to see the Church of God as in the first days, when the Apostles spread their nets to take, neither gold nor silver, but men." '[1]

The name of Miguel de Molinos has no place in the Roman Calendar, but he cannot be omitted from the roll of Spanish Mystics. The 'Quietism' which he taught had many advocates in France, and among those who were persecuted for holding his views on the contemplative life were Madame Guyon and the saintly Fénelon, Archbishop of Cambrai.

> Two worlds are ours ; 'tis only sin
>   Forbids us to descry
> The mystic heaven and earth within,
>   Plain as the sea and sky.—KEBLE.

[1] See *Les Mystiques espagnols* (Paul Rousselot).

PRINTED BY
SPOTTISWOODE AND CO., NEW-STREET SQUARE
LONDON

Date Due

Ap 2 6 '40		
My 8 '40		
O 2 7 '40		
1 '40		
My 1 7 '43		
F 5 '48